Lallia
(Le Cow-boy)

Lallia

(Le Cow-Boy)

DJANET LACHMET

*translated from the French
by Judith Still*

CARCANET

First published in Great Britain in 1987 by
Carcanet Press Limited
208-212 Corn Exchange Buildings
Manchester M4 3BQ

Carcanet
198 Sixth Avenue
New York
New York 10013

The publisher acknowledges financial assistance
from the Arts Council of Great Britain

I should like to express my warmest gratitude to Dr J. Collie, Mr S. Daniels,
Ms N. Brick, Dr A. Brown and Mrs C. Still for their help in reading and
discussing this translation.

British Library Cataloguing in Publication Data

Lachmet, Djanet
  Lallia.
  I. Title II. Le Cow-boy. *English*
  843'.914[F]   PQ2672.A235/

  ISBN 0-85635-563-1

Typeset in 11pt Garamond by Bryan Williamson, Manchester
Printed in England by SRP Ltd, Exeter

I was sitting on a bench at the end of the alley, searching through my dress (which was brown, dotted with white flowers) to see if I could find the four-leaf clover which would bring good luck to my new house. The sun was high in a sky so blue that even the trees began to look blue. It wasn't hot and the March morning wind was good for the blossom coming out on the apple trees whose scent was slightly bitter. The gate was open, we were moving house.

I felt slightly sad for my other house which I'd left behind. Whenever the removal men went by, I put my hands over my cheeks and watched them carrying in the furniture. I didn't want to look for the clover in front of them because they would have seen my underwear, which wouldn't have been right. So I thought about the old house, two storeys high, opposite the mosque next to the church. It had a big green wooden door decorated with huge nails, always closed on a long corridor which was scarey at night. But whenever the sun invaded the courtyard, you could see the patterns of the wrought ironwork on the balconies dancing even on the door.

A removal man came up to me with something in his hand.

'Is this yours?'

'Yes, that's Boudi.'

'And what's your name?'

'Little red pearl.'

He smiled and patted my head.

'That's a pretty name you've got there.'

'My grandmother gave it to me.'

The man turned round and went off, and I hugged my fish Boudi to my stomach.

Boudi, you remember the washing day when I got drowned. Yes, of course you remember, you were born then. I was almost two. My mother and Mamessa, my second mum, weren't there, and the woman who was hanging out the clothes on the terrace wasn't watching what I was doing. I was playing in the courtyard, pretending to wash Dad's handkerchief, and I stood on tip-toe like the woman who dances at weddings, and my head made me fall into the tub full of water. Mamessa told me that I was dead for ages. I was pulled out by my feet, you do remember, it was after we moved with Mamessa to Rhômana, you came with me.

I'm glad you're here. All my old toys stayed in the box room. I wonder what will happen to them. Perhaps Mamessa will unlock the big padlock and give them to the children of the blind beggar who comes every Thursday.

Why didn't Mamessa come with us to the new house? Its bound to be Mum making trouble for her because of me. Ever since they brought me back from Rhômana to go to school I've not been allowed to go off with her on her travels. Whenever I see her she won't stop crying. And I'm sad too not to be with her, but I'm afraid to tell Mum that.

I was born with spots on my tongue like small white flowers. I was very ill and they even thought I might die. My mother was suffering, and so the doctor told her to stop breastfeeding. She wanted a boy. My father had promised Mamessa that she would be my nurse if I was a girl. She waited for the birth praying that I would be a girl. She secretly prepared things for me, and God answered her prayer. When I was born I was a girl.

Mamessa took lots of herbs so that she would produce milk and one day it came. Everyone said that it was a miracle, a sign from God. It was written that Mamessa should look after me and bring me up. She was very happy, she'd never had any children and longed to have some. At last I stopped crying, I was breast-fed and even my tongue healed.

So I was Mamessa's daughter and I travelled about with her. When we moved to Rhômana, my mother was annoyed with Mamessa and didn't speak to her for several days. She was jealous of her and didn't like to hear me call her my 'dearest Mamessa'.

My real house was at Rhômana. I spent the day following the ants who were going to find food, and in the evening Mamessa would tell me stories. Sometimes, when it rained, I would fall asleep in her arms. She would sit on the rug near the fireplace and watch the devil burning in the flames. No one could disturb me there.

My second dad spent his evenings in his prayer room with the holy texts of the Koran. He was Mamessa's husband, his beard was completely white even though he wasn't old. When he looked at me I always thought he was crying, but his mouth smiled. In the morning when he left for la Medersa where he taught, I used to install myself at his table and, wrapped in a piece of white cotton like a h'baia, I played at being my second dad. At the end of the day, when the sun had not quite set, he would walk with me in the orange and lemon groves. The raucous birds would follow each other like shadows. I would follow their path in the sky as they made patterns and arrows. I would collect lime blossom which Mamessa dried to make herb teas to soothe fever, and I'd go back to the house looking like a hunchback, my apron filled with medlars and cherries, and round my neck a garland of pomegranate buds, which opened up like lace.

Bent over his low table, my second dad would be immersed in the sacred histories. I used to spy on him through the narrow opening of the door, keeping watch on his every move, thinking perhaps he would look up and call me. The desire to run and throw myself into his arms would make me impatient. I would try to calm myself, waiting for him to look at me. Then, tired of waiting, I'd make some little sounds, scratching at the door like a cat so that he would know that I was there, that I wanted to come in. Then he would raise his head and, through his small glasses, look at me and smile. I would wait a bit, then I'd come closer, first slowly, then running to press myself into his arms which were already open and waiting to gather me in.

Mamessa would tell me stories of sad princesses pursued by misfortune, and, walking through the orchard hand in hand, my second dad would teach me the story of the Prophet. When I was tired of the story I would pretend to be sleepy and he would carry me in his arms, then I would close my eyes and try to hold back the laugh of happiness which I felt inside and which made my eyelashes tremble. He would believe that I was really asleep and bring me back to the house clasped against his chest. He would put me down in my little bed next to Mamessa's big bed, then I would open my eyes and stretch my arms out towards him. He would lean over me and I could see in his eyes that he was happy. He would stay there for a few moments, his head against my heart, then he would cover me up and go out of the room. Then Mamessa would come,

10

sit next to my bed and go on with the story she had begun the day before. Then she would settle under my head my little pillow embroidered with yellow chicks.

When there was a festival, all three of us would go and visit Mamessa's family, at her elder brother Sidi Abdeslam's house, at Zaouïa. Sidi Abdeslam had a frightening voice, but his smile was famous. People came from all around on pilgrimage, bringing precious offerings for the saints, and they would settle in for the week. The women visited the dead, lamenting the departed. They would go off, clusters of women in white under their veils which were blown about by the wind. Some of them would arrive at the mausoleum in a trance. They would light candles and burn a mixture of djaoui and henna. Smoke would rise and a mysterious perfume invade the fields, which smelt of pines and cypresses. Those women would tie multicoloured silk scarves to the branches of trees, while others, who wanted a son, lay down on the ground to have their stomachs massaged by the cheikh's wife. Old H'lima would already be installed under an oak tree, receiving the women one by one, to explain their dreams to them.

The men would go out at night, they prayed out loud in a chorus led by the cheikh. Every day the servants would cut the throat of a black bull for sacrifice. The women who cooked would bustle around by the stoves, enveloped in steam and smells from the big cooking pots. The women who made the couscous worked on the semolina, sitting, legs apart, with their wooden trays in front of them, telling stories to each other. The young girls, pleased to be together again, would talk of love.

The meals took place outside in the meadow. Carpets were spread out and the men were separated from the women by a vast white sheet held up by stakes. And so a white wall puffed out by the wind cut the countryside into two. Anxious newly-weds would try to meet each other all along the wall which stretched right down to the river; it was patrolled by boys because such meetings were forbidden.

I used to get frightened by the men on horseback shooting, while the women, who'd already made lots of holes in the sheet so that they could see, spurred them on by their whooping. I would cry when occasionally someone was hit by a bullet. I never went near the horses, I would go and see the lambs and comfort them. Perhaps their mummys and daddys had been killed to feed the guests. Several sheep were slaughtered every day. They would plant stakes for the grills and then the sky would change colour. The smoke made clouds which looked like a dirty ceiling.

In Mamessa's bedroom a woman was packing the blue trunk on which painted fish swam amongst the waves. The black car would come and, if Abdeslam would drive us, we'd go via Rhighia and stay a couple of days with my parents.

I jumped and shrieked with joy in the courtyard, I was going to see my daddy again. Through the car window I saw the forest go by and the branches of the trees waved at me. The pines smelled good. My face in the wind I breathed in the smell so that I could remember it afterwards.

We'd just come into town when Mamessa woke me up. I felt sick and my head ached. I recognized my sister Fafa in front of the door to our house, going in and out, all excited. I wanted to be sick, the road had been very twisty, I don't like cars, I prefer horse-drawn carts. I had hardly got out of the car when Fafa began to annoy me.

'You look all yellow, your dress is creased, tell your Mamessa to change it.'

I knew Fafa, she wanted to make me take off my dress so that she could try it on. She dragged me by the arm, I couldn't even struggle because the journey had tired me out so much, she showed me to my mother who, as usual, pretended not to be interested. She looked at me as if I were the monkey in rompers which gets shown in the market on Wednesdays. Mum came up to me with a distant smile and gave me a brief kiss. Fafa wouldn't leave me alone. *She* was interested in nobody but me.

'You're putting on your fine airs, don't think you're not. I've got a pretty dress too, *much* prettier than yours.'

'So what, you haven't got a princess's outfit, like the one Mamessa made me.'

12

'Oh the show-off, a princess's dress!'

'Yes, like Loundja, you don't know that story, *and* you haven't got a fluffy white winter coat.'

'Does it snow in Rhômana?'

'Yes, and the snow in Rhômana is much whiter than the snow where you are. In the morning, the robins come into the courtyard and call to me between the window bars, they perch on the branches covered with snow like cotton wool. The sun warms them up, but the branches begin to cry because they don't like the sun-beams, and their big tear drops fall and make holes in the snow in the courtyard. Then I go out, in my fluffy coat, to look at the stars which fall from the sun on to the snow... you see, you haven't got a white coat.'

'Tell me some more; what is there in your Rhômana, and then I'll tell you.'

'About my red boots?'

'No, tell me, or I'll get angry.'

'I put seeds and pieces of fat on the wall for the robins, I sing about the white snow, white on the roofs. Then I help my second dad to clear a path.'

'And then, go on.'

'Then, I go in, my nose is red, and my eyes hurt because of the bright light.'

Fafa dragged me into the corridor where it was dark, and then disappeared leaving me there. She came back covered from head to toe in a sheet, pretending to be a ghost. I shrieked in terror, I was always afraid of the dead coming back. Fafa hadn't changed. I knew very well that it was her, but I was still afraid. She deliberately made me fall over and I got bruises all over my thighs. When Mamessa complained to my mother about her, my mother said to her: 'Tie your daughter up, she's a whiner.'

I ran and hid under the sideboard to punish them. The mothers, when they heard little noises, thought that there was a mouse in the sideboard. So they sent the cat in who didn't find anything. They said that he was good for nothing. Annoyed, he went and hid under the bed.

I did better in the linen cupboard – it's big and they couldn't

13

hear me. Daddy's clothes had a lovely smell of amber. Mamessa would look for me, and say as a joke: 'I think that the little red pearl has gone off with the beggar.'

In the morning Fafa came and woke me up, whispering to me: 'I am the mouse who nibbles your ears.'

Startled, I leapt up and cried out, and I was the one who got scolded. When Mamessa goes to visit her friend I shan't stay at home, I shall go and see Dr Maler, he teaches me songs and explains to me how the hands go round and make the time on the round watch.

Dr Maler lived next door, I would go through the garden gate and I'd be there. He was the one who'd brought me into the world. He would often ask me to mimic my mother, and so I would put on a deep voice and with a strict face order Fafa to do something. I would also tell him the story about Mamessa's feet, the big toe who was in charge and the little toe which was tiny and was always late for school.

Then I would tell him how Mamessa tied me to the door handle with a piece of string so that I wouldn't do anything naughty. She'd give me piles of rags to make dolls with. I would stay there, tied up, and Fafa would come and ask me to bark like a dog otherwise she'd take my dolls away. She also told me to put on my fine airs, but I can't do it when I'm tied up. So she would give me a slap and go off. Sometimes I managed to undo the string and escape into the courtyard. Mamessa would catch me and lift me up in her arms.

'Tell me: why are you so small, why are you so beautiful, why this and why that?'

'It's to make trouble for you, Mamessa' (I would say that to her as a joke).

Mamessa would hug me to her and I'd see tears fall down her cheeks. Then I'd be sorry.

'Why are you crying, Mamessa?'

'You can cry when you're happy, I'm crying because I love you so much that I'd like to eat you all up.'

'I want to go into your tummy too, through the little hole in your tummy.'

14

When I had a temperature, Mamessa would put me into the copper bed. I'd turn the knobs which made faces look bigger, and I'd talk to the bars, which reminded me of women in sarouels. It was Mamessa's marriage bed, it had a little arched golden door and a key on a chain. You got up into it by stairs covered in pink satin. It was like the saints' koubba.

'Mamessa, why didn't you move this bed to Rhômana?'

'It's too heavy. And then this is my home too, we often come back here.'

'I like Rhômana best, because Fafa isn't there.'

'You're very fond of your sister, she plays with you and teases you.'

'Yes, but why does she hit me?'

'She's a bit jealous of you, its always like that when you're the smallest. Anyway you're coming back with me to Rhômana soon. And remember that you often ask if you can come back to see Fafa.'

I was collecting the dead leaves which were beginning to fall in the courtyard, when I saw my second dad go through into the house. I was taken aback to see him so early. I followed him inside, he was looking for Mamessa to warn her that my father was arriving that same morning. I was so pleased at the thought of seeing my father again that I jumped up almost to the ceiling.

Mamessa got me ready and made me beautiful. I couldn't keep still, I went to and fro in front of the big mirror, looking at myself, admiring my shoes and my dress. I kept talking at top speed and no one could understand what I was saying. All out of breath, I kept coming in and going immediately back out again to look for the arrival of a horse-drawn cart, being very careful not to get dirty. I couldn't even play, I gathered up my toys as fast as I could manage and threw them into a corner. I waited, I waited ages, I waited so much that I got tired and had a headache. Perhaps it was the perfume which Mamessa put on me that made me feel ill. I went to the kitchen to get a drink and I spilt the whole glass of water on my dress. I was so furious with myself that I gave myself a scolding.

'What's wrong with you, is your lip split?'

I heard the noise of wheels and ran outside. The cart had just come into the drive at the end of the orchard. I wasn't sure whether to run and meet him or if I ought to change or what. Mamessa was in front of the entrance, her hand on her forehead to protect herself from the sun which was bothering her.

'The red pearl is like a dog with two tails, isn't she Mamessa?'

'Are you happy to see your daddy again, my poppet?'

I calmed down when the cart stopped, I was a bit better

16

behaved. My father got out; he had brought Yemna back, the woman who helps Mamessa, she had been on holiday with her family. Yemna is very nice, I'm very fond of her, she's almost a grandmother and yet she jokes with me, and we do silly things together when Mamessa isn't there. She lets me do anything and she gives me piggyback rides. She cries sometimes when she gets told off by Mamessa because of me.

Yemna carried all the packages inside and then my dad could put his arms around me.

'How big you've grown, you deserve a real school satchel now!'

He kissed me, kissed Mamessa after he'd put me down and we went into the house.

'How's Lalla Smâa, how's so and so, how's...' asked Mamessa.

Meanwhile I was eating sweets. Fafa had sent me a whistle and a picture as a present. I neatly folded the transparent papers of all different colours, which smelled of violets and raspberries. I ate all the sweets, only leaving the caramels which I gave to Mamessa so that they wouldn't spoil my appetite.

After dinner my father and my second dad had a talk in the sitting room. Mamessa was sad and kept looking at me while she was clearing up. I followed her from room to room and I thought I could see tears in her eyes. She turned away and put her hand over her face.

'Are you crying, Mamessa?'

She didn't reply but knelt down in front of me, then put my head on her shoulder and held me there against her. I shivered: it was as if someone had walked over my grave.

'Are you crying because you love me?'

Mamessa looked at me and I couldn't hold back the tears which were streaming from my eyes. I swallowed them quickly and I couldn't understand why I was crying so much. In bed Mamessa calmed my sobbing and then went back into the sitting room. On my own, quite still, I didn't sleep. I was scared.

I took Boudi out from under the pillow and, when Mamessa came back to see me, she took me on to her lap and gave me her breast. I hesitated a bit before taking it, because I was a bit old, and it makes you stupid, but I overcame that feeling and sucked almost in spite of myself, forgetting that I was six years old.

'I don't want to go away with daddy, I want to stay here with you.'

Mamessa, surprised, tried to hold me close. I pushed her away.

'Who told you that you're going away?'

'I just know. Daddy's come to fetch me, hasn't he? Tell me, it's true isn't it?'

Mamessa didn't reply; so I pulled myself violently free and ran to the sitting room, I pushed the door open and loudly announced:

'Don't bother, I shan't go away with you, go back to your daughter Fafa, I'm my second dad's daughter.'

My father tried to catch hold of me, I ran and hid under my bed.

I refused to have anything to eat at breakfast. Mamessa washed me in silence and I wouldn't look her in the face. My father told me stories which I pretended to listen to.

'We shan't leave for another two days. You'll go to see your mummy and Fafa and then you'll come back. I'll take you out this afternoon if you want. Would you like that?'

'Yes.'

I looked beautiful. Mamessa had put pink hair-slides in my hair. I was happy to be going out and I forgot to feel miserable.

'Daddy, the horse blew in my face.'

My second dad kissed me and hugged me tight. So did Mamessa. I jumped into the cart and sat down on the bench. I waved to them till we got to the end of the drive.

'See you this evening Mamessa, I'll bring you back a beautiful bunch of flowers.'

The cart went out onto the road and the horses' shoes clattered on the tarmac.

'It's very pretty here, Daddy, isn't it?'

A family of birds came up close to us. I could almost have caught them. I put my head on my dad's knees and I swung

18

my legs along the seat, my white socks had a pretty pattern of holes, but they were a bit tight. The cart moved with a steady rhythm and after a while I dropped off to sleep.

I dreamed that I was in a train with Mamessa. I went out into the corridor to look for the toilets and when I came back I couldn't find Mamessa's compartment any more. People were jostling me, they were in a hurry and no one took any notice of me.

'Where are we, Daddy?'

The cart went into a small town, taking the main road lined by two rows of plane trees, a gallery of leaves screened the fronts of the houses. I didn't recognize a thing. It was beginning to get dark and I was still half-asleep. Then the lights in the houses began to come on one by one, and I tried, as we went on, to find something from the back of my memory.

We came towards a square. I thought then that I recognized the town, the town where I was born. This was the square, a deserted square with a man who waters the flowers around the statue of a soldier with a moustache, his head held high and his rifle on his shoulder. That was it, the war memorial. I'd been tricked.

I felt so bad that I wanted to be sick over and over again. I cried and cried: I was inconsolable.

I wanted to stop crying, but I couldn't. It was completely dark when the cart stopped in front of the house. I struggled, I refused to get out, I clung to the seat with all my strength and nobody could tear me away from it.

My father, sad and exhausted, went into the house, leaving me with the driver to whom I clung desperately, begging him to take me back to Rhômana. I held on to his jacket, which was wet with my tears, I didn't want to set foot on the ground again.

'Take me to Mamessa's.'

'Tomorrow. I'll come back and I'll take you back to Rhômana. It's dark now, you can't see to drive properly.'

I didn't believe anyone any more, I would keep my misery to myself, I hated the whole world.

My mother was angry and blamed my father. Fafa was nice

19

to me for once. But the red pearl was miserable and didn't want to eat anything any more. She wasn't hungry. She thought about her dear Mamessa who was waiting for her bunch of flowers. I wouldn't cry any more in front of them, I pretended that it was all over but, when they weren't there, I would secretly think about you Mamessa, and about my second dad. I'll never forget you. Boudi cried with me too.

Dr Maler came, because I was feverish, and I told him everything.

'Daddy stole me from Mamessa who is waiting for me to come back with some flowers.'

My mouth was on fire, my eyes were stinging, my lips were dry and bleeding. At night I had terrible nightmares. A big black dog with yellow teeth and a great big mouth dripping with blood was chasing me. I ran quickly into the forest, at top speed, and I tried to climb up into the trees, which made fun of me when I wanted to climb. They got higher and my hands slipped on the bark. The dog got nearer and, at the moment when he was going to catch me, I woke up shrieking, my face drenched, I thought that he was under the bed.

'I'm thirsty, I want a drink.'

I looked amongst the sheets for Boudi and I clung to him. He was drenched too and feverish. I was allowed to have my light on all night, I looked at the angels hand in hand on the ceiling. I didn't want to go back to sleep.

School had started again. In the bookshop there were lots of children with their fathers, each awaiting his turn.

I had chosen my satchel myself. Fafa had given me her slate, and I had pieces of chalk in every colour. I put some letters on the slate, which I showed to my dad to see if I'd made words which meant anything. Dr Maler had taught me the alphabet.

The school wasn't far from our house, and you could hear the big boys playing football on the other side of the wall. At the entrance I gripped my father's hand tightly and didn't want to let it go again. I was afraid of getting lost amongst all those children. Fafa put on airs in front of Dad to show that she was grown up. When she saw girls she knew, she introduced me to them saying: 'This is my little sister.' I mimicked her and made fun.

My overall was the prettiest. I looked at the little girls who were crying, clinging to their fathers' legs. *I* was pleased to be going to school, I wasn't crying.

A lady came and opened the big wooden gate, and called out the names. When she heard hers Fafa ran and lined up with the others. I would have liked to go with her, but it wasn't my turn; I would be called too.

The teacher came up to us and stroked my hair.

'What a good little girl not to cry.'

She took me into the classroom and, as I was the smallest, she put me in front, at a desk with a white inkwell. When the bell rang, I met Fafa at my classroom door. She was waiting for me so that she could protect me during playtime.

I worked well at school and the teacher always gave me good marks. Dr Maler had brought me back books with pictures of France in them. I knew the story about the grasshopper, and I could sing the song about the ant. Every Thursday I went out on a walk with my teacher. She taught me the days of the week and what a year is. I knew Winter, Autumn, Spring and Summer.

In June, at the end of term, all the schools, even the boys' school, put on shows at the town hall. The big girls in the sewing-room made the costumes for the little ones. Their school was just next door. They often came to get me in the middle of lessons so that I could try on my costume. As they undressed me they played with me and tickled me under the arms.

I learnt my dance well and my teacher was pleased. She showed me off to the inspectors who came to visit us. They said nice things to me. I knew my song off by heart.

The performance was that evening. After lessons, my teacher took my hand to help me cross the road. The day before my father had taken me to the hairdresser's to get my hair cut, and I had gone to the baths. I was so clean I shone like a new pin.

There were already lots of children at the town hall. They filled the corridors with noise. A gentleman with a tie went by in a great hurry. He had a basket in his hand; perhaps it was the Deputy Mayor. Another gentleman went up the stairs carrying a chair. I got dressed the first because I was the first one on.

When I was ready I left to make space for the others who were still being dressed. There was no one in the hall yet. I went up to the big mirror on the wall and admired my costume with its white net petals. They'd put a wire thread covered in braid round the edges so that the petals didn't droop. I adjusted my gold belt because it kept slipping down on to my hips. They hadn't made it tight enough at the waist. My top was a bit short and too open over my bare chest. Fortunately I didn't have any breasts at that stage. Assia, the girl who sat next to me in class, had the beginnings of breasts. They were like two big broad beans, very hard.

My sandals were annoying me, the straps left traces of gold

dust on my legs. My cap was very pretty, like fish scales when the sun gleams on the fish in the water.

I was suddenly surprised by a blond head appearing in the mirror, and I felt embarrassed at being watched. I turned round and couldn't see anybody. But the brim of a hat had just disappeared behind a pillar. I went up and discovered a boy hiding there. He looked at me with a smile as if he were making fun of me.

'What has he got to snigger about?'

I glanced in the mirror to check my outfit in case anything was wrong.

'No.'

He came closer and pulled a revolver from his belt. I thought he was really stupid.

'What are you supposed to be?'

'Can't you see? I'm a daisy.'

'A daisy? You don't look like one. You might be a butterfly with those wings.'

'Have you ever seen a butterfly with petals?'

'Oh they're petals! Now you tell me.'

'Are you chasing robbers?'

'No, I'm a cowboy from the Wild West.'

I thought he was insufferable.

There was a badge on his hat in the shape of a bull's head with large horns. He was wearing a checked shirt and a small triangular handkerchief. His suede trousers had fringes which came down to his feet. He had a big patterned belt and two revolvers. I looked at the cowboy and I didn't like him at all. He wasn't polite and I was even a bit cross. He took my place in front of the mirror and made himself look interesting by lowering his belt to around his hips. His boots had a heel like women's shoes have. He would show off when there were girls around. I started to leave, abandoning him there. He ran and caught me by the shoulder.

'You're very pretty.'

Then he ran off like the wind to the other side. I went back to the mirror and I thought I looked pretty.

Then all the other girls arrived.

23

'What are you hopping about like that for?'

'You've got a different costume from us, you've got practically nothing on.'

I thought to myself that perhaps being a daisy wasn't quite nice.

They were jostling each other in front of the mirror in their deep red, almost black, satin. Like the flowers from a Judas-tree. They started practising their steps, getting in the way of the teachers who were putting up boards to make the wings. I helped arrange the chairs for the parents, putting them to face the platform where we were going to perform. We hid behind the boards so that the guests couldn't see us. The hall gradually filled up.

My group was opening the show: the lights went out and the guests took their seats. The girls were fidgeting and trying to see if their parents were really there. Then the last noises died away and the music began.

In the darkness, the daisy crouched down in the middle of the platform; only a point of light was visible. The roses came in three by three, like fine ladies, and surrounded me. I got up slowly and acted as if I didn't know where I was. My arms rose up with the music as the light spread. The roses did arabesques around and around me trying to prick me. I danced to avoid their thorns. Suddenly I didn't know what to do. The boy from a minute ago was there, behind the curtain, he was looking from the side. I felt myself blushing, I was ashamed, my stomach was bare, you could see my navel. I couldn't remember any more what I had to do, perhaps that boy was laughing at me. I wanted to stop, to run away, I felt like crying.

The teacher saw that I was upset and came up to the platform. She whispered the next bit to me and I felt better. I found the rhythm again and the words came back to me. I didn't look over towards the cowboy again.

The end. It was dark and I bumped against my schoolmates as I got into a line to take my bow. When the light came up again, I recognized my dad and Dr Maler sitting in the front row. They were clapping. I rushed into the wings where the teacher took my photograph before undressing me, then I went back into the hall. I was going to laugh at the story of the cowboy and his Indians too.

Lallia, red-cheeked, got up. She had been sitting watching the removal men for a long time. She picked up the bear which they had dropped and went back in, taking her little bench with her.

In the house everyone was busy. Crockery was lying around on tables. Furniture was spilling out into the courtyard, the rooms were in a mess. After the meal she went to bed, her bed had been put at the end of one of the bedrooms. She didn't know this house very well, but she'd already found her own niche. She would do her homework on the terrace, which had views over beautiful countryside right up to the railway line. Raredj, the stork, was back in her nest on the roof of the house opposite.

Lallia also knew the children from round about, who already came to fetch her at teatime. They would go round the memorial together on their scooters, and when night began to fall she would go home all out of breath.

Yves, the son of the neighbours from across the alley, used to come and play with her in the park. His parents lived in M. Brosoli's house, the architect who went off to live in France.

Lallia had noticed Yves and his sister on the day he arrived. She had watched their comings and goings, not leaving the terrace all day. The two children had looked up at her and smiled. She thought they looked nice and waited for a chance to speak to them.

That evening, as custom required, her parents would invite the newcomers to dinner. So she seized her chance.

'I'll go and tell them, mum dear, let me go, please.'

She did her hair and, thrilled, ran towards the door.

'Calm down, do you even know what you're going to say?'

'Good-evening, Madame, my mother would like to know if you and the family would come and eat with us this evening.'

'You should say: "It's a tradition. The first day you move in you never have to cook. The neighbours take care of that."'

While their parents were drinking tea, Yves and Lallia were getting acquainted in the square. She asked:

'Where did you live before?'

'On a farm, we came here because of school and also because of the bandits.'

'Because of bandits?'

'Yes, the bandits who live in the mountains and who come down at night to rob houses. They stop people who're on their way home and attack them.'

'Have you ever seen them?'

'No, I haven't, but my father has. He even spoke to them one night. They held up his lorry by standing in the road with torches.'

'Did they attack him?'

'No, they wanted to know who he was.'

'And so what did they say to him?'

'I don't know exactly, my father told us that they weren't real bandits.'

'I haven't lived here long either, we're new in the area too.'

Yves and Lallia met every day after school. They became great friends.

'Do you know René, the boy from the park? We're in the same class.'

'No, I don't know him.'

'He knows a great game, but you need three to play. Do you want to join in?'

'What sort of a game is it?'

'You'll see, it's a surprise.'

At the park entrance a love-apple fell on Lallia's head. She looked up. In the tree a boy, astride a branch, was turning aside so that she'd think he had nothing to do with it. He jumped down and she recognized the boy she'd seen at the school show.

'René, I've found a third.'

27

'A girl?'

'That doesn't matter, we'll explain it to her.'

'What's your name?'

'Lallia.'

'I'm René.'

'I know.'

'Good, listen carefully! Yves and you, for instance, choose the name of something either from the park or from the road and I have to find out what it is. You can help me by putting me in the right direction, but without telling me anything. I ask you questions. You reply with a yes or a no. Do you understand?'

'Yes.'

Yves and Lallia went off while René covered his eyes with his arm and leaned up against the tree. Then they came back smiling.

'O.K., you can look.'

'Is it in the park?'

'Yes.'

'Can you eat it?'

'No.'

'Does it roll on the ground?'

'No.'

'Can you throw it?'

'That depends.'

'No, no, you've got to reply either yes or no,' said Yves.

'No.'

'Is it green?'

'Yes and no.'

'Is it yes or no?'

'Yes, but it's got two colours.'

'Is it yellow too?'

'Yes.'

'Mimosa.'

'No. You know you can only suggest three things, then you have to give up.'

'Does it have a third colour?'

'Yes.'

'Does it have a smell?'

'Yes.'

'Does it have petals you can pull off?'

'Yes.'

'A marguerite?'

'No.'

'I've got it! It's a daisy.'

'Well done! You've won.'

'Why did you choose a daisy? Couldn't you think of anything better?' said René.

'Last year I played a daisy in the school show at the town hall. That's why.'

'Yes, I remember. Were you the daisy? Well, you haven't changed.'

'I recognized you straightaway.'

'I've still got my cowboy outfit, I still put it on sometimes.'

'I don't know where my costume is any more, it got lost when we moved.'

'Do you live round here now?'

'Yes, opposite Yves's house.'

'I live there, at the end, behind the courthouse. My father's the judge.'

Lallia loved playing with the cowboy: she met him every day, they spent hours together. When they fell out, Yves sorted it out. René got cross easily and didn't like to lose. He was spoilt by his mother because he was an only child.

On Thursdays Yves and René did their homework together. Lallia would spend the day in one of her parents' shops. Djilali, the man who looked after the shop, found her a place behind the shop where she could work. It made a change from home. When she was tired she went into the shop and dealt with customers.

René often went away with his mother. He had written several times to Yves – letters and cards – but he'd never sent anything to Lallia.

'Has René written to you?'

'Yes, a card of the place where he's staying, it's by the sea. Do you want to see it?'

'No, I was just asking.'

'He sends you his love. Do you think about him a lot Lallia?'

'No, I'm not in love with him, only why doesn't he write to me?'

'I don't want him to.'

'So you're stopping him from writing to me?'

'No, I'm teasing you; if you like, I'll write to you myself.'

'I'm not interested.'

'Do you love him? You must tell me.'

'It's none of your business.'

'But I love you.'

'I don't want you to love me, you always try to make me kiss you, and you cry when I don't want to.'

'Why don't you ever want to?'

'Because I don't feel like it.'

'And if René asked you?'

'Never, anyway I'm never going to speak to him again, he's a show-off.'

'Liar, you're saying that now, but when he comes back you'll forget.'

'This time you'll see.'

René didn't want to play with girls any more, he was always with boys. Lallia walked across the park. She pretended to be out for a walk, hoping that he would speak to her. He ran past without stopping. She went home and found a letter on her bed. She tore the envelope open, but the letter was from Yves. Furious, she went to find him.

'Are you mad or something? You write me this, a love-letter, and you put it on my bed. Do you want my parents to find out? Don't ever do it again!'

'I'm sorry, Lallia, I just wanted...'

'You just wanted, look what I think of your letter.'

She tore the letter up and threw it into the gutter which flowed past the door. Yves watched the bits of paper as they separated and he tried to put the words together again as the little stream was slowly carrying them away. He bent down, collected them one by one, and went home in tears.

Lallia regretted her action and her anger, but said nothing

to Yves.

'If I say something he's going to go on thinking that I love him, he'd believe anything. I'm miserable, and I can't even say a kind word to him. He keeps forcing me to be nasty. I hate him. I can't even have a laugh with him without him thinking that I love him. And then, that mournful puppydog look...'

Lallia decided to write to René.

I'm miserable because I never see you, you've gone away again. Yves goes on being a nuisance when you're not there. He even told me that you've got a girlfriend there, where you go on holiday. But my kisses are for you and you only.

The daisy

Yves threatened Lallia from his window. He pointed to the mercurochrome on his elbows and the bandage on his knee. She didn't understand why he seemed angry, it wasn't her fault if he'd fallen over. She hadn't even been there.

'What did you say to René? Do you want to make trouble between us? Are you happy now, we've fought and we're not talking to each other any more. He got hurt too, we fell on to the gravel, his knees are scraped even worse than mine are. He got punished by the teacher, all because of you.'

'I have to tell someone that you're being a nuisance; I can't talk to my father about it, we decided not to tell our parents about anything that goes on between us. Isn't that right?'

'I didn't tell my mother that I'd had a fight. I told her that I was running and I fell over.'

Lallia walked out to school, hanging her head. The cowboy startled her by shouting in her ear.

'You frightened me.'

'I meant to. Were you counting ants?'

'No, in fact I was thinking about you.'

'You know, I saw the postman put an envelope in the ninth hole of the third red brick to the right.'

'It must be Yves again.'

'Shall we see each other later?'

'Will you be with the others?'

31

'Yes, of course.'

She got up to the pile of bricks, waiting to be built into a wall, and took out the envelope which had been slipped into the hole.

Daisy,
I liked your letter. I taught Yves a lesson, he won't make a nuisance of himself again. I don't have a girl-friend when I go away, anyway I'm not interested in girls.
The Cowboy

Delirious with joy, Lallia carefully hid the note in a book and went out to meet the cowboy. In a corner of the square the girls were playing in a circle, shouting out the song:

Rosi, Rosa, I love you, I love you
Rosi, Rosa, I love you as you are
I've chosen the loveliest
To be my partner
I've chosen the loveliest
The love of my heart.

René was playing tag with the others. Lallia sat down at the foot of the war memorial and read the names once again:
Bertrand Carpentier, Fell in battle, aged 27
Zaoui Djaffer, 33, Died for France.
René ran out of the road, scarlet-faced, chased by two boys on the other side who ran round him and tried to grab him. He ran back, they did the same, then he charged forward and got through them. Without stopping he pulled off his jumper, ran towards Lallia, threw it at her and ran off again. He'd escaped them.

Lallia picked up the jumper and hugged it to her. René arrived, breathless, he'd won. He sat down next to her to have a rest.

Yves was still angry. He was walking around on his own without speaking to anyone, his hands clenched in his pockets. The cowboy joined him, catching hold of his shoulder. Yves backed away and went on walking.

'Let go, leave me alone!'

'O.K., if you're going to take it like that.'

'You know, what you've heard is a load of rubbish!'

'About what?'

'Lallia. I'm not speaking to her any more.'

'Come on, she's the one who told me to come and get you.'

'Well, of course, who can she complain about if I'm not there?'

'Lallia, give Yves a kiss on the cheek and let's forget it.'

The three friends went back to playing together as before. That evening, Lallia opened her book and re-read the cowboy's letter. She repeated it to herself, tomorrow she would show it to Rida, her friend at school. Every evening she wrote poems in an exercise book for the cowboy.

I opened my eyes: it was still dark. A face was bent over me.

'You're awake, go back to sleep, it's too early for you.'

'I'm cold, Dad.'

'Wait a minute, don't wriggle. I'm going to cover you up, you always throw your covers off.'

'What time is it, Dad?'

'It's time for the dawn prayer, you can go back to sleep.'

I woke up bit by bit, nice and warm under the covers, and everything came back to me.

'Ah! right, it's today that we're going off to stay with our grandparents. School's over, it's the Easter holidays. I'd completely forgotten that I'd packed my things yesterday. I chose my red dress with the white collars for the journey. I tied a ribbon onto my hair slide, I'm wearing my white sandals and taking my gym shoes to wear there.'

I heard the outside door, it must have been Dad setting off for the mosque. He would bring back doughnuts and bring in the milk from the doorstep. If Mum wasn't asleep she'd get up before he got back, bring in the milk herself and get breakfast ready. Then she'd come and wake Fafa and me. I washed. Dad didn't like it when you came to the table without having washed, especially your face. He said that it was disgraceful to eat with your face still sleepy. We're not animals. Yves and the others had breakfast before they washed. I was glad that I didn't eat breakfast with them. They would have frightened me with their eyes half-shut and their sleepy mouths.

I got up, the house was sleeping, I crept out on to the terrace. The sky was still dark, but with a touch of blue. That night blue, mixed with light. In the distance, a crack appeared in the sky and the sun peeked through, his face still pink. He sent out sunbeams like the hands on a big clock to chase away night and sleep. The coolness wasn't from the wind, the wind was still asleep and the trees weren't stirring. You could hear a cock crow in the distance, like the muezzin calling to prayer. I went downstairs: in the courtyard the fountain was burbling like amorous doves. Its voice was so familiar that I only noticed it when I saw the water. My father had washed; he'd forgotten his watch on the side of the basin.

I was shivering in my thin, almost transparent shirt.

'What are you doing out here bare-foot?'

I hadn't heard my mother coming and I stopped in surprise for a moment.

'Nothing. I can't sleep. Dad forgot his watch.'

'Go back to bed.'

'Let me stay with you, Mum dear.'

I rubbed against her legs like a cat. My mother was very tall. I could never reach up to touch her face, it was as if she was always standing upright. She was straight-backed, almost stiff. I took her hand and rubbed it against my arm to warm myself up. I was so happy to be on my own with her. That morning she let me carry on for a bit, she even smiled at me. I played at being a tiny little girl to see what her reaction would be. She didn't say anything, she didn't push me away, she was passive. Perhaps because she was going to see her own parents. She was remembering when she was small.

'Mum, you know, it was Dad who woke me up, I was dreaming.'

I hopped around her, I wanted her to notice me. She looked at me, perhaps I interested her that morning. I'd never been so happy before.

'Stop hopping, you're like a swallow who's getting ready to fly away early in the morning.'

'I'm cold.'

'Go and put some slippers on, don't stay out here with bare feet.'

I ran into the corridor. There was Dad, who'd just come in. I jumped up, put my arms around his neck and wouldn't let go. He tried to get free, but I stayed clinging to him like a monkey.

'Why aren't you in bed? You're going to make yourself ill.'

I was so pleased to be going to the country that I spent half the night telling myself stories. My grandmother still called me the little red pearl, and my aunts never told me that I'd grown. They used to pick me up in their arms like a baby, and I loved being a baby. My mother always made fun of me because of that, and she would make me cry with her scornful looks and words. Yet I worked well at school, I was always top of the class. But Fafa worked well too. She was always top too, and besides she didn't play any more. She was like the big girls.

I remembered everything my grandmother told me.

'You know that your name is the name of a great lady,' she told me, 'it's my mother's name. She was also called the wise one. She used to write poems for her children, and the men of the family would consult her when they had an important decision to make.'

One day I too would write poems for my children. At that time I wrote for the cowboy and for my grandmother.

My dear Mama, my sweet Mama,
I love it when you call me Mum and you put your perfume on me which no one else has the right to wear. I love it too when you call me the little red pearl and you show me all the jewels in the case which your mother gave you. I like being in some way your mum. I still think all the time about what you tell me.
'Pay attention to the man who makes you cry.'
'Beware of the man who makes you laugh.'
'Life is a corridor which may be long or short. Some go through it with their eyes closed. Others strain to see in the dark. Some go through it with their eyes open but without seeing.'
I often keep my eyes open in the dark and I try hard to see something. Perhaps I could make light come. For those who are in light go to paradise, the others are on the path to hell and yet they don't know it.

36

My grandmother said that paradise was when you die. *I* thought that paradise was on earth and that the sky was its garden. And when you're grown up, if you deserve it, you go to the end of the world, and there, there is a stairway which goes up into the garden. I thought that hell was in the desert, very fiery, under the sand. One day at school I saw some little animals who'd died in the desert. They were hollow because the fire had eaten out their insides. Only their carcasses were left. The teacher explained it to us.

I shall go to paradise, because I'm not wicked and I work hard. I never say rude words. I shall wear my beautiful white *Aïd* dress and I shall go up the stairway at the end of the world. I'll find Mamessa, my second dad, and you Mama and everyone I love. When I look up at the stars, I think that it's the good Lord who's lighting the candles so that he can see those who're misbehaving down below.

The sun was completely up. It was blinding, even through the pine trees. I sang out of the car window, and the wind carried my words away. I clung on to my father's neck, he was sitting next to the driver, I hugged his neck fiercely.

'I'm so happy that I'm afraid that my heart will fly away like a bird.'

'Dad, why do we die?'

'So that we can go to paradise.'

'I want to be a swallow to find out what it's like, perhaps the end of the world isn't far from Mama's house.'

My mother opened her veil and took my hand away from my necklace.

'How many times do you have to be told not to put your chain in your mouth?'

My jewellery was made by M. Isaac. The rabbi from the synagogue wrote a charm for me against the evil eye so that no harm would befall me.

When I got home aunt Matti would bring us matzos and the cakes she'd made for the festival. Although she was Jewish, aunt Matti didn't always wear black like the rabbi's wife. Even the rabbi's daughters, who were my age, were always dressed in black. They never went out of the synagogue where they

37

lived. They were twins, as like as two peas in a pod. I used to think that they were waiting for the return of the great saint that God made disappear on the river bank when his enemies were after him. When he comes again, we'll have paradise on earth. There'll be no more wickedness on the earth, nor beggars, nor madmen. And the twins and their mum won't wear mourning any more.

From time to time I would go and play with the twins in the synagogue courtyard. A strong smell of incense would fill our nostrils. I loved listening to the chanting in the ancient tongue. Loud and solemn voices would float out of the windows and go up to the heavens through the leaves of the tall trees which surrounded the synagogue. It would upset me, the voices seemed sad, sometimes they scared me. The men who went to the synagogue on Saturdays wore hats as black as the picture frame in the sitting room. They also had black beards and ringlets like English girls' which fell on to their shoulders.

Fafa used to frighten me at night by imitating the synagogue chanting. She would take some cardboard which she rolled up into a funnel and speak slowly into it.

'We are the men in black from the synagogue, we have come to fetch Lallia.'

The car came to a stop at the side of the road at the edge of the pine forest. Two men on horseback came to meet us. Dad and I got out to say hello to my grandfather and my uncle Nadir. A khamass was holding a horse saddled for Dad. Uncle Nadir lifted me up with one hand and, without getting down from his horse, he put me in front of him. Mum got up behind Dad. Fafa wasn't there. Too bad. She'd chosen to go to my other grandmother's.

That evening it was the henna festival. My aunt was going to get married. She was sitting on a cushion, I could see her smile through her veil. She was surrounded by women decked out like princesses. I was passed from arm to arm, rubbing against the women's perfumed bosoms and touching their clinking jewellery.

The children were all outside and I hurried to say hello to

38

everyone so that I could go out. The little ones were playing on the swing, the others were playing at weddings. Two boys, perhaps my cousins from the capital, were showing off with rifles. They were shooting at birds, I thought they were wicked.

When she was small my mother used to play with her cousin Nadir. He used to kill birds too. He was an only child and his father spoiled him. He would take him hunting with the men. One day when he was on his way back from hunting, my mother, who was, as grandmother said, also a curious little girl, provoked him and made fun of him. She kept saying to him that he didn't know how to shoot, that he was afraid of the hares and the rabbits, that he wasn't even capable of killing a sparrow. Uncle Nadir, who was only a bit older than she was, got angry. He threatened my mother with his gun, but Mum, sure of herself, went on scoffing at him. Uncle Nadir shouted: 'Stop it, Saliha, stop it or I'll shoot.' My mother was very cheeky, and she pushed him right to the edge. So Uncle Nadir shot at her and hit her in the shoulder. Even today she still has a slight scorch mark on her right shoulder.

Once one of my cousins wanted to teach me how to shoot and I wounded a bird in the wing. The bird thought that I was a good little girl and had perched just next to me on a bush. He was turning his head, quite unsuspecting. My cousin was helping me hold the rifle because it was a bit heavy, he kept saying press, press the trigger. I pressed and the shot rang out. When I saw the bird fall, I screamed, I was very unhappy. I picked him up and carried him into the house. He wasn't dead, but he was in great pain. I found a box and made it into a nest. I put fine straw and down into it. I gave him some food, but he didn't want to eat. I tended his wound with spirit and ointment, and then one day he died. I arranged a service to mourn him. I tore up an old sheet for his shroud, and I sewed it myself. The khamass's son made a coffin for me. His sister knew how to mourn the dead. She asked me the name of the bird so that she could mention him in her lamentations, I called him Safsaf.

He was buried in my grandparents' cemetery, near our

ancestral mausoleum. I put chaheds and flowers on his grave. I went to see him every time I came for a visit. On Fridays I watered his tomb. I shall never touch a rifle again.

My other cousins were playing weddings again. It was always the same. The girl cousins were the brides and their male cousins the husbands. They would dress the bride, and make her up with matchsticks dipped in colours, and she'd wait inside the hut with her face veiled until the boy cousin came in. The others stayed outside. The girls danced and sang and the boys would go with the groom to the hut door and then push him violently inside. He had to pretend to be embarrassed. Then he'd put the wooden plank back in its place as if he were closing the door. He'd lift up the veil and kiss the bride on the mouth and they'd fool about together. The girls outside would whoop and the boys fire their rifles in the air like men do at real weddings.

I would refuse, I wouldn't play those games any more. I didn't want to be dishonoured. If I played at being a bride, I would lose my virginity. Like that poor girl from the mountains who played with her cousin when she was small, and when she got married properly she wasn't a virgin. Her in-laws were furious and disowned her. They put her on a donkey, facing towards its tail, with her head shaved and her arms tied, and they took her back to her family. Her elder brother stabbed her to death because she'd dishonoured her family.

When I stayed with the women I was spoiled and cossetted. I didn't go out to play silly games. After the evening meal, the old women would gather all the children round them in front of the big fireplace where the cat and the dog slept, and they'd tell us stories about the Prophet and his companions. But I preferred the story which my grandmother told me about the family.

My grandfather had an uncle who was called the scholar. He lived shut up in his library which led into his bedroom and his sitting-room where all his meals were served. Only one person was allowed to enter his apartments, and that was his young serving-maid. She was deaf and dumb and was devoted to him. She was, so they said, exceptionally loyal.

In his bedroom he had had a marble bed built, it was hung with panels of material embroidered in gold instead of curtains. He immediately pulled these curtains across if someone managed to come in unexpectedly, which didn't happen very often. If someone did, the powerful odour of a wild animal would catch in their throat. Someone was sleeping in that marble bed, covered with tiger skins and woven cushions, but everyone pretended that they didn't know who it was.

'Who was in the bed, Grandma?'

'Patience, little one, I'm coming to your bit.'

Grandfather's uncle, my grandmother went on, decided one day that he wanted to get married and asked Lalla Smâa to choose him a bride of noble blood, like himself. The marriage took place without any kind of ceremony. He was then about fifty years old and his wife barely half that age. After a few months, on a night when the moon was full, the whole household was awoken by shrieking. The cries came from the scholar's apartments and nobody dared to interfere. Then all became quiet again and everyone went back to bed, except for one servant who was told to keep watch near the scholar's apartments. It was the scholar's young wife who had cried out.

The next morning the servant had disappeared. No one ever knew what had become of him. Great curiosity was aroused by a freshly-dug grave, discovered a few days later in the family graveyard. As no one in the family had died, they imagined that the scholar had killed the servant and had buried him himself, against tradition, in the family cemetery. The servants had their own burial place and so it was decided to move the grave and to keep the matter silent.

But when the men dug up the corpse they were filled with amazement. The dead person wasn't the servant whom they expected to find, but the scholar's young wife, wearing her wedding dress and all her jewels. She seemed to have been strangled. The body was put back in the grave and no one said a word.

No one could speak to the scholar. He would reply to no one. He imposed a supernatural respect on all those who came near him. He was feared, and no one dared do anything against

41

him. After that dreadful episode Lalla Smâa died of unhappiness. Every night the men watched around the scholar's apartments. They feared further mishaps.

Every full moon, the men saw the scholar go out accompanied by a she-panther wearing hanging earrings. Her paws were covered in red leather shaped into little boots. The scholar talked to her as he walked and she replied. Those who saw them said that she spoke men's language and had a woman's voice. At the next full moon an old woman from the family was summoned to follow the scholar and the panther on their nocturnal walk. The panther answered to the name of Bahya, the very name of the wife who had died a few months previously. The old woman also recognized the dead woman's voice.

Using hidden cracks in the roof, they tried to spy on the scholar and the panther's solitary existence. The panther sat opposite the fireplace on a large leather foot stool, listening to the scholar reading aloud. They recognized the earrings encrusted with precious stones and the thong of plaited gold which the panther wore. They were jewellery which had belonged to Lalla Smâa the scholar's mother.

Rumours were running through the district like a plague of locusts. Some claimed, swearing by all the saints, that Bahya the panther was the scholar's mother. They said that Lalla Smâa loved her son in more ways than a mother should, and that while she was alive she had shared his bed. She had strangled her daughter-in-law, of whom she was horribly jealous, and then she had poisoned herself. After her death she had turned herself into a panther, usurping the young wife's voice in order to deceive her son who was consumed with grief.

'Is that true, Grandma? Did the noble Smâa really do that?'

'No, little one, you'll hear many other versions, but this is the truth.'

Lalla Smâa, of noble birth and of noble character, did indeed die of sorrow after the death of her daughter-in-law. She thought that her son had gone mad. The death of Lalla Smâa left a gap that only the following generation succeeded in repairing. Both men and women were affected by her absence for a very long time; they could not be consoled for as long as they lived. Lalla Smâa was a great lady, generous and wise. We call upon her, oh God, on the merciful night of Achoura, that her greatness and her goodness may flow down upon us and upon all her line down to the last born.

My grandmother was lost in thought in front of the fire's glowing embers for a long time. I didn't dare interrupt her meditation although I was eager to know the end. I moved closer to her, took her hand and pressed it to my lips. I was torn between a strange feeling of pride – because I was descended from Lalla Smâa – and a feeling of awe and terror which made me shiver.

'What happened to grandfather's uncle after that?'

He lived for several years with the panther Bahya, who, according to some, was his mother, and to others, his wife. And one night, the same kind of sleepless night as his wedding night, under the full moon whose features were distorted in pain and whose mouth was open in a scream, the roar of a savage beast, followed by a great din, was heard. The beautiful panther, the noble Bahya, was tearing the body of her faithful husband apart. She was not to leave the least fraction of a limb. She was to lap up the last drops of blood. When they got into his apartments, Bahya had disappeared. No trace of her was ever found.

But ever since, on the night of a full moon, people have heard the desperate roaring of Bahya the panther.

'When is the full moon, grandma? I should like to hear Bahya.'

'It's much better not to hear her, my child.'

I went past the boys' school one more time to see if the cowboy was there. I hadn't seen him since I'd come back from holiday. The boys went in through the big wooden door. I recognized some of them, but the cowboy was nowhere to be seen. I searched the road thoroughly, but there was nothing. I heard my school bell ring in the distance, I started running: I was late. I came across the headmistress in the playground, she gave me a reproachful look. I ran past as fast as I could so that she didn't have time to call me back.

The lesson had begun and my classmates were as silent as the grave, as if they wanted to make my lapse even more obvious. I got over my uneasiness and went up to the teacher's desk.

'I'm sorry, Madame, I overslept.'

'Isn't there anyone at home who can wake you up?'

'...'

'Very well! Go and sit down!'

I went back to my table with some of the girls in my class looking disappointed. They would have liked me to have been humiliated. Especially the class dunce. She was the oldest. She always tried to win the teacher's favour by wiping the blackboard. Every time the teacher dropped the chalk she would rush to pick it up.

'Close the window,' the teacher might say, 'it's cold.'

And Zakïa the dunce would spring up with a threatening air as if to say that it was *her* job.

'Will someone please hand out the exercise books?'

Again it would be Zakïa who went up and down the rows, saying a few spiteful words as she went, flinging the exercise books of the girls she didn't like to the ground.

She was very ugly, like a mangy monkey. But her parents

were so poor that sometimes she would cry in class because she hadn't had anything to eat. Then we would feel sorry for her: we'd bring things for her and club together to pay. She was the poorest in the class. It was a shame that she was so horrible.

In the art class, I wrote poems for the cowboy and drew the head of my second dad with a long beard and glasses. At that time I used to get bored in lessons. Sometimes I wanted to cry. I felt miserable when I thought about Mamessa's smile. I didn't like drawing, I doodled on the paper and then got fed up and tore the piece of paper up.

The teacher had changed. She punished us all the time. Before she used to joke with us, and tell us a bit about her life. Now she got angry very quickly and tore up our work if it was badly written or if there was the slightest mistake. The girls told stories about her. Zakïa said that her fiancé had abandoned her, that he'd gone off to France.

'Lallia, show me your drawing. Out you go, you lazy girl! A bit of air will do you good.'

She showed me the door. So much the better. I watched the birds fly away from the courtyard, perhaps they were going on a long journey.

'If you're going to Rhômana, tell my second dad I love him.'

Every time that someone went through to go to the toilets, they went past our classroom door. Each one gave me a long hard stare as if to embarrass or make fun of me. They looked me up and down. Even the religious instruction teacher I'd thought was nice.

The week before Safia had got the dunce's cap. The teacher had pulled Safia's pants down and hit her with a heavy ruler making red stripes across her buttocks. They were swollen for several days, she couldn't even sit down. Safia's mother came to tell the teacher off. She asked her if she did the same to the girls from French families or if that kind of punishment was reserved for the little Arab girls so that they'd be discouraged and not want to go to school. Safia's mother was red with anger, her veil nearly came off, and her mouth was covered in spittle. The other girls laughed at her behind their satchels.

45

I even quarrelled with Annie Vignot because she was making fun of the woman who didn't speak very good French. She mimicked her, mispronouncing words.

Yolande, who sat next to me in class, came and told me to come back in. The teacher had sent her to get me. I'd been outside for three hours. Meanwhile the others had been working on their verbs. I wasn't very pleased since I enjoyed that lesson.

It was the end of the school day. The cowboy was waiting for me by the gate. I thought I must be dreaming. He was craning his neck to find me amongst the crowd of girls who were milling around. Yves was there too. I looked for Rida and took her arm in a tight grip.

'Stay with me, *please*!'

'What's wrong? Are you scared of Zakïa?'

'No, you know, that boy René, I've told you about him, he's there, he's waiting for me with Yves.'

And without looking at them, I went on dragging Rida with me. Yves came up to me.

'Let's go on, Yves, don't talk to me here in front of the others. You can both of you pretend to go on on your own, Rida and I'll follow you.'

'But what's wrong?'

'Go on, I'll explain to you later.'

I was in a state, I was scared, shaking, I felt as if all the other girls knew what was going on.

'Rida, I'm so happy, René's come to get me from school.'

'You're happy? So why did you send him away again?'

'I'm scared of the others, of Zakïa.'

'That's silly.'

'I don't like people calling me names.'

Gradually the other pupils disappeared. Yves and René went ahead up the road to the cemetery on the outskirts of the town.

'Who are you afraid of, Lallia?'

'You know, Safia hates the French. Last time she told me that I ought to be ashamed to go around with them. She saw me in a shop with Yolande.'

'Come on, don't think about it any more.'

46

Rida caught up with the two boys who went on walking and I thought about the long trip which had separated René and me. Then the story of his girlfriend came back to me. I looked at René who was slowing down, leaving Yves with Rida. It was a beautiful day. Without making a decision we did something unusual, we left the path which led home. We got to the top of a hill. On the tennis courts, two grown-ups were sending the ball back and forth – it made a noise on the surface like a bird tapping its beak. It was the daughter of the town bank manager and her boyfriend. He was on leave from his military service with a parachute regiment. As he played he leapt as if he were still up in the sky.

Yves and Rida pressed up against the wire netting, silent and well-behaved, following the game. René and I sat down under the sacred oak, which was surrounded by fire-blackened stones on which the women burn *djaoui*. René opened his satchel and handed me a package, all wrapped and sealed with an exercise-book label on which he'd written 'Daisy'. I looked at him and he looked away in embarrassment. He picked up a stick and drew crosses in the earth.

I tried to undo the paper which was wrapped round a circular box. On it was painted a cowboy with a daisy between his teeth. I was deeply touched.

'How did you find it?'

'I had it done on holiday by an artist, my mother's cousin.'

'It's great.'

'I wanted the cowboy to be lying down on his stomach looking at the daisy, but he wanted me to have this. Which would you have liked best?'

'I like both. Oh look, you've got a butterfly on you.'

René followed the butterfly while I opened the box and took out two red hearts wrapped in cotton wool. On one heart was written 'you' and on the other one 'me'. At the bottom of the box there was a piece of paper folded up small. I unfolded it: it was a drawing of a daisy. On each petal there were nice things written. René came back with the butterfly.

'Let it go, René, it doesn't like being like that.'

'Look at the powder it's left on me, it's like gold.'

'Did you do the daisy or was it your mother's cousin?'

'I did it and I did the writing.'

'It's lovely, it's...'

I didn't know what to say, I was so happy. As for him, you'd think he'd done it just like that, for a laugh. Perhaps he was sorry he had, he didn't look happy. I ran off to find Rida, leaving my treasure there, open, underneath the tree.

'Rida, come and see, what should I say to René? He's given me a lovely present.'

Yves went over towards René who jumped on him and began to grapple with him like a real wrestler at the circus. Yves struggled a bit and then attacked him in his turn.

'You know what you should do – give him a kiss.'

'But how do you mean? Kiss him on both cheeks like with Yves?'

'No, kiss him properly.'

'On the lips?'

'Haven't you ever kissed anyone like that?'

'No, have you?'

'Lots of times.'

'Don't you lose your virginity?'

'You're O.K. as long as you just kiss, it's when you do more than that that you lose your virginity.'

'I'd never dare. It's boys who start.'

'He gave you the present, so you must kiss him.'

'Is that how it should be?'

'Yes.'

'René, René,' Rida shouted. 'Lallia has something to tell you, she's behind the tree.'

Oh dear! What a mess she's got me into now.

René came over to me, all out of breath, his shirt open, his jumper twisted round and his trousers covered in dust.

'You've lost some of your shirt buttons.'

I stayed with my back against the tree not daring to move. René looked at me and came closer. Then he put his arms around the trunk, I was his prisoner. His face was so close that I held my breath. He was still breathing hard because of the fight. He squeezed me against the oak tree and kissed me.

Yves and Rida were behind the tank of the water tower playing with the echo. René held my hand and we went home. I told him the story about the man who killed three spirits: they came for his wife every evening and carried her off into the forest. The man was very jealous, and one night he decided to wait for the spirits in a thicket. He was armed to the teeth and he was so angry that he killed all three of them. Afterwards it turned out that they were real men and that one of the three was his wife's lover. She was sent away.

'Do you get scared when people tell you stories like that?'

'No I don't get scared, anyway, I don't like stories.'

'After we've stayed up late listening to stories I can't sleep, I stay awake thinking and that gets me scared. When I hear noises in the courtyard, I burrow down into the bed and hold my breath.'

'So why do you listen to these stories?'

'I like it, I snuggle up to my mother and then I feel safe.'

The next day I went off with the cowboy to his parents' farm. I told my parents that I was going on a school picnic and Rida helped me deceive them.

The cowboy's farm was beautiful. He had a horse with white markings on its russet coat. He had a tree-house made out of reeds, perched up in a poplar as if it were a home in the sky. You got up to it by a ladder. There was furniture inside, a table to do his homework on. There was also a mattress for his siestas.

The farm was surrounded by fields, and when we walked through the corn not even our heads were visible. You could play hide and seek and would keep getting lost.

The Thursday before I had visited the rabbi's daughters. As there was no school picnic I'd chosen to do my homework at the synagogue. To get to their house I had to cross the market place where the weekly cattle-market was in full swing.

Country people came to it with their sheep and goats. Rows of little donkeys were tied up in front of the entrance, having a rest while they waited for their masters. On market day the main gateway was opened. There were so many people you could hardly get through. Sometimes I liked getting lost among the crowd of men. Some would stand, others lean on their animals, holding them by the neck. Some would slip from place to place, from group to group, bargaining. Others, stuck in the middle, shouted to attract people's attention.

A number of corrugated-iron shelters with zinc roofs had been built on top of the hill in order to protect the meat. It was the main butcher's shop for the market. Sheep, kids, lambs and even gazelles were sold in quarters. The headless bodies were cut up and hung by their necks. Fresh blood dripped down and darkened the dry earth which absorbed it instantly.

The sun beat down upon the hill which was enclosed on

every side. It was as hard to get out as to get in. Cries rose above the heads, blue and white gandouras bleached by the sun moved about and the breeze made the cheches balloon out. Some children tried to make their way between the long tanned bodies of the country-folk. The frightened lambs could sense that death was near. I stroked a kid whose eyes brimmed with tears. It made me feel ill and I had to hold back my anger. Then I ran off, leaving behind me the powerful odours of flesh and sweat.

Finally I reached the avenue which ran alongside the synagogue. It was protected by the shade of the mulberry trees and the planes. It was cooler here. The country folk often came here to rest when they left the market, their faces burnt, their veins green and swollen with heat.

There was no shade on the market-place. It was waste ground, enclosed by rusty iron railings, which was opened up once a week. Hooligans tore out some of the railings so that they could get in when there was no one about. That was where they met to get up to no good.

On the pavement along the avenue there were grocers' shops with low entrances which opened into dark rooms. As you went by you could just make out silhouettes behind the narrow counters. The smells of pepper and cloves mingled with other fragrances. A sugary cinnamon taste came into my mouth. The breeze brought one smell which dominated the others, an odour of burnt caramel, which reminded me of something – I searched for the time, the place, of that memory without ever finding it.

There was a bench in front of one of the shops. A holy man was sitting meditating as he told his beads. Children bent and kissed his hand, which he would mechanically hold out. A cup of coffee on a copper tray was placed on the bench next to him. He put his hand to his brow and looked up at the patch of sky visible between the leaves.

When I'd finished working with the twins, I went over towards the mosque to wait for the end of prayers. There, in the garden, the immam, all in white, sat in the shade of a medlar tree. He was reading the Koran in a barely audible voice.

My father came out. Slightly put out to find me there, grumbling, he took my hand. Then he kissed me on the forehead and we went to the shop together. I filled my pockets with sweets which I handed out in the evening in the war-memorial square.

Behind the mosque there was a souk, where all sorts of wares were displayed on squares of canvas spread out on the ground. A man called out the virtues of bottles of red and green liquids, cures for all maladies. A snake-charmer sat cross-legged in front of two wicker baskets, the lids off, where curled up snakes were sleeping. I slipped between the men's pleated trousers into the front row. A tight circle had formed around the baskets.

He played some swift tunes on his pipe, and the snakes' heads slowly reared up, their eyes open and their gaze piercing and unwavering. They stretched up swaying from left to right like pendulums, in their gold robes spotted with black. 'It's a couple,' someone said. I tried to guess which was the female, and recognized her by her elongated eyes, with two black lines as if she was wearing kohl. Her head was finer and quite triangular, with a pointed tongue which came out at the speed of lightning and vanished like a spark. The male had more spots on his coat and his head was wider. Intimidated and frightened, I lowered my eyes because I had the feeling that the snake was looking at me and ordering me to lower them. Then I wanted to hold my own and looked at him without faltering.

A man was sitting nearby. He was playing cards and seemed elsewhere, his eyes turned inwards. He told incredible tales, he didn't call out to people, instead he held out his hand and the person felt drawn in spite of himself. He concentrated on the queen of spades. His square, laid out in front of him, was held by four large stones. Near him there were old pictures of legendary saints and pages from the Koran. One showed Sid-Ali and his two sons Hassen and Hocein. The other, a devil with a sword in his hand and bulls' horns. He was threatening a child with his sword.

The blue and green picture was of Bourak, the mare with a woman's head, magnificent with her mane of black hair. Her

52

slim muscular legs arched into the sky, her wings were fully extended. In the desert there stood a wise and upright man, his hands by his sides, his head high, his soulful eyes inviting you to pause. A lion lay tamed at his feet, his paw on one of his master's feet. The sky behind him was like a web of blue light touching the carpet of golden sand by one thread.

Another picture reminded me of the one in our sitting room. It was of Abraham's sacrifice. Abraham was on a mountain top, preparing to lay out his only son on a stone slab, to cut his throat. His hands were tied behind his back. Abraham was going to kill his son, as God had ordered him in a dream. In the sky the loveliest of all the angels, holding a ram, was ordering Abraham to let go of his son and to seize the animal which was behind him. This was how Abraham was rewarded for his obedience to God and, since that time, the faithful have always killed a ram in memory of that occasion.

Someone behind me cried out: 'It's America!' I turned around. A group of people were standing round a mountain of odd-looking clothes. They gave off a strong smell of second-hand clothes shops; the country people laughed at the whale bone which stuck out from the old evening gowns which smelled of the theatre and of mothballs.

A bit further on there was a table where thousands of bottles the colour of honey, the blue of the islands and sun yellow, were tightly packed into wooden cases. The man made his own perfumes. He took petals out of bags and then mixed them. And so you got essence of musk, jasmin, amber and rose. He sprayed the passers by and the whole souk exuded a smell which gave you a headache.

I made my way back to the church square which wasn't far away. The doors were closed, the sun was very heavy, a storm was threatening; I glanced at my old house, I didn't miss it any more. I had dawdled too long. I was going to get another scolding. My mother would say: 'She's possessed by a devil which drives her to go and hang around dirty, crowded places.'

My mother often worried; she thought that my solitary walks were peculiar aberrations. She even thought that I was possessed by demons. But I preferred to be beaten than to give them up.

It was tea-time: I arrived covered in dust. The whole family was gathered together, they weren't even waiting for me any more. I was so thirsty that I didn't listen to the grumbling.

'Why didn't you wake me up?'
'Because you were asleep.'
'How long have we been here?'
'I imagine it must be hours.'
'It's very hot here.'
'It's time for a siesta.'
'Have you slept?'
'A bit. I've mostly been thinking.'

René pushed open the door of his tree-house and covered his eyes with one hand while with the other he held on to the rungs of the ladder so that he could climb down from the poplar tree. It was very hot in the tree-house and outside the sun made you screw up your eyes. As soon as he was down, René rushed to the pump. Finally he got a huge jet of water from it. Each of us in turn crouched down and was sprayed from head to toe. Then we went into the barn to dry off.

René had undressed. He walked about in his underpants, shaking his hair in front of my face to send drops of water on to me. Naked, I wrapped myself in a sheet which was lying in a corner of the barn. Then we climbed up on to the straw to play at outstaring each other.

I thought about my parents who believed that I was on a school picnic. And what if they learned that it wasn't true? What if I'd been stupid in coming to the farm? What if lying was serious? What if God wanted to punish me?

'René do you know the story about the two sisters?'
'No, tell me.'

There were two sisters, one who always told the truth, and one who always lied. The first one was nice and clean and polite – everyone liked her. The second was dirty and sullen and obstinate and didn't speak to anyone. She always stayed at home. She'd been rejected and so she rejected others.

'Which do you think told the truth, the first or the second

one?'

'The second.'

'You reckon?'

One day the second sister went to the spring to fetch water, her dirty hair rolled up in a filthy scarf. She plunged the bucket in and the handle slipped from her hands. She began to weep, to weep over her misfortune and, seeing the water become calm and limpid again, she bent down to see if her bucket was within reach. She met a very beautiful face which got larger as she got nearer to it.

'Who are you, beautiful lady, a being of this world or a being from beyond? Human or otherwise?'

'I am the sister who tells the truth.'

'I too have a sister who tells the truth, she is beautiful and well loved.'

'Bend down further, put your hand into the water, take the mirror which is there and go home. Look at yourself for a long time and let it speak to you. Then give the mirror to your sister.'

When the mirror had spoken to her, she gave it to her sister and the mirror said to her:

'Who comes to consult the dirty sister, to make her truth their own, who disguises the truth with guile and deceives the innocent?'

'What is that mirror saying? It's mad, what does it mean? I'm going to smash it!'

'Truth is the prisoner of someone with no virtue who constantly repeats to the other that they will always be beaten. But the time for the naked truth always comes, when artifice and guile are useless.'

No one could understand what was happening: that sister began to shriek and insult the mirror. Instead of words she spat out toads and serpents from her mouth. Maddened she ran out into the street, shaking herself, but the animals continued to crawl down her skirt. People turned round in surprise. The second sister picked up the piece of the mirror which the first one had smashed, and vowed to help her.

'I was right, it was the second one.'

'Yes, you were right.'

'But why did you tell me that story? Because you've been telling lies?'

'No.'

At home no one noticed my falsehood. I invented details about the picnic, even stories about the other girls and the teacher. I'm always convinced that it's the last time I'll ever lie, and I always do it again because of parents who never let us do what we want.

The cowboy had gone off again, he hardly came to school any more. His mother made him work at home to catch up with the lessons he'd missed. He didn't like school much and said so. I got bored at school too, especially now that I had a new teacher. I was with the big girls who wore make-up and dressed like women. The dunce Zakïa was still in my class and she still got at me. I had to give her money and sweets or else she'd hit me and tear up my exercise books.

I didn't work hard any more. I was no longer top of the class. My parents weren't very happy. In the last school report I got zero for conduct. I was a chatterer, and I always got punished.

'Gharnad, will you bring me your homework, have you got it with you today?'

'No, Madame, I've forgotten it again.'

'Miss Gharnad, do you think I'm a fool? Get out!'

The headmistress went past the classroom door at that very moment.

'You again, Miss Gharnad?'

She pulled my ear so hard that I was afraid it would come off in her hand. I felt humiliated and I touched my ear to see if it was bleeding. I waited until she'd gone into another class-room and then ran off. The gate was open. I felt as if I were on top of things when I was on the streets again. I made my way towards the water tower. There, by a vaulted door, deco-rated with a copper hand, a little hunchback was begging, her head pressed against the closed door.

'Oh! You who love God, Oh! You who are believers, alms in the name of the Lord.'

I went up to her and she turned around.

'I know you, you're called Lallia.'

'Yes, you're right, but I don't know you.'

'I live at Mr Humpert's, my father takes care of his farm.'

'Humpert's, of course, I know them, they've got an entrance on the alley near us but they don't often use it.'

'Yes, our entrance is below, on the railway side. We live in with the animals.'

The hunchback was wearing an old dress which had belonged to a grown-up. You could tell by the flounces decorating the top. A woman must have given it to her as charity. She'd cut off the bottom so that she could wear it.

'I've run away from school.'

'Oh! Dreadful.'

'Don't you go to school?'

'I went once, but I don't want to go again. I've no clothes and my father won't buy me anything. He says he hasn't got any money.'

'Have you got any sisters?'

'Three sisters and two brothers.'

'Do they go to school?'

'No they don't. Every time we want to enrol them there's no spare places. My mother says they don't want to enrol us because we're poor, they say we're dirty.'

'Have they given you anything at this house?'

'They haven't even answered.'

'Have you tried anywhere else?'

'I don't feel like it today, I'm not being very lucky. I spent the whole morning washing the pavement in front of this French woman's house and she just gave me a piece of cheese spread. I'd rather have some money for my mother.'

'Here I've got some money, it was for a girl in my class.'

'Thanks. Do you want to come with me?'

'Yes, I can't go home till school's over.'

There was a huge dung-heap where ducks and turkeys played, a vast opening like a cavern with rotten planks of wood, then we went into a passage where our feet squelched in the mud. A hen came clucking in, followed by her cheeping chicks who invaded the whole of the entrance right up to the back

58

where the cows were lying. On the right there was the one room where the hunchback and her family lived. A fire was lit in a large black fireplace. The room was full of grey smoke. You could hardly make people's faces out. A skylight let in a square of daylight divided by the iron bars.

A warm and serious voice, slightly hoarse, said to us:

'Come in, children, come in.'

I couldn't see anything and I was afraid of squashing the chicks who were running between my legs. I found it hard to adapt to the darkness, but, bit by bit, as she pulled up a bench on which she'd placed a cushion, the mother's features became clear. In place of her nose there were two enormous quivering holes. A large brown beauty spot sat like a cherry stone, on the corner of her mouth. Her lips were thick and curled back showing large teeth blackened perhaps by the smoke. Her smile was heartwarming, her eyes sparkled with kindness and tenderness. She was a large lady, plenty of flesh, with generous bare arms protruding from their sleeves. Solid arms which would envelop you like a hen with her wings.

'What are you called, dear?'

'Lallia.'

'You see, here we cook on a wood fire in the fireplace. We don't have a stove. Your eyes aren't used to the smoke, don't rub them, you'll be all right. It's this wretched wood which is damp – it's out in the rain all winter long. The farmer won't let us use the wood from his cellar. He keeps that for himself. It's a dog's life for us, dear.'

She said it all quite merrily and made me laugh myself.

'Are you laughing at your aunt Adda's way of speaking, dear?'

She went on talking as she added pieces of damp wood which she took from a bundle in the corner of the room. My eyes were stinking and tears ran down my face. I began to feel cold, but I didn't dare move from the bench. The hunchback sat, legs apart, in a corner of the fireplace to warm herself up.

'Get away, Keïra, you won't be able to move from there if you stay too close to the fire.'

'Keïra, how do you sleep?'

'We spread blankets out on the raffia mat, we lie side by side and hug each other to keep warm.'

'And your father and mother?'

'They sleep with us, by the door, we sleep by the fireplace.'

'Aren't your brothers and sisters scared at night?'

'Sometimes my brother wakes us up. He dreams that he's fighting.'

The hunchback's sisters came in, rubbing their hands together and blowing on them. They threw themselves into their mother's arms as she sat cross-legged. There was plenty of room on her lap. She hugged and kissed them noisily. She said sweet things to them. She calmed them down, cajoled them, defended them. Even the hunchback rubbed up against her although she was older, fourteen: it was her hump which made her look small; you'd think she was about nine. I didn't dare ask her if it had been an accident or whether she'd been born like that.

I often went back to the hunchback, Keïra's, place. We became friends. Her mother was very fond of me and would hug me to her bosom as well. She always made me a place next to her around the djefna at mealtimes. I ate with my fingers sitting on the ground leaning against her as her children did. Aunt Adda's cooking was excellent. She would cook mardoud with pieces of dried meat in a big soot-blackened pot, it smelled delicious.

When Keïra's father came home, he'd take one child at a time on his lap because he was skinny and there wasn't much space on his lap. Sometimes he would grumble at them with a voice which came from way high up in his head. He was so kind that I wanted to run and put my arms round his neck too.

Aunt Adda loved the farmer's cows, she spoke to them as if they were human.

'My lovely big red girl, you're tired, you're still giving milk to your sturdy little calf, he's wearing out out, you have to eat. Take this my pet.'

The chickens and their chicks would waddle into the room. They loved being with us. They would walk about and dip into the dishes, climbing up on the blankets which got piled in a corner every morning when the family got up. The chicks would cheep and look for their mothers who pretended to hide. Then the cock would arrive, pause for a moment in the entrance as if to see what was going on and then suddenly fly on to the fireplace and shout cock-a-doodle-doo.

I would take things from home, hide them in a bag and go out when there was no one in the courtyard or in the garden. I would take them to Aunt Adda who was delighted.

Sometimes Keïra would come and meet me in the square and would stay and play with us. At first my friends weren't very nice to her, but not for long. She didn't much like playing anyway, she preferred to watch us run about. I would go and talk to her and stroke her cheek from time to time. Now my friends brought her what they could steal from home. She didn't wash ladies' floors any more, we gave her parcels which she came to fetch from the war-memorial square; those who didn't bring anything were thrown out of the gang.

Keïra, the hunchback, had an aunt whose husband was away in Germany, he was a soldier in the French army. Keira asked me if I would write him a letter since her aunt couldn't find any one to do it. The hunchback's mother came to ask my mother's permission. My mother felt sorry for Aunt Adda who told her about all her misfortunes and about all her sister's misfortunes, and she let me do it.

Keïra's aunt lived on the outskirts of the town, on the road which led to the Jewish cemetery. She looked a lot like Aunt Adda, except that she was younger. The poor woman had a stiff leg and a crooked foot. She sat me at the meïda and covered it with an oilcloth with big yellow and red flowers on it, which had been neatly folded in a cupboard. She treated me like an adult which made me feel a bit awkward.

My father was pleased that I was being helpful in this way, and he gave me writing paper and envelopes. Only he didn't want me to go to her house to write. So the hunchback's aunt came to our house once a month so that I could write a letter to her husband. I got used to writing to this gentleman in Germany. When he replied it was me he addressed. He kept telling me that he was very happy to have regular news of his

61

family at long last, and I, for my part, felt that I'd known him for years. He told me jokes in his letters to make me laugh. He sent me parcels which I gave to Keïra because my father didn't want me to accept any presents.

I took some photos of his children. The man in Germany was thrilled. He even said that he'd wept. He hadn't seen his youngest for five years. She'd been born while he was away.

I enjoyed being with the hunchback's family. But my mother didn't like it. She poked fun at me: 'Go and live with them since you like them so much, I saw you crossing the square yesterday with your arm round the hunchback, are you afraid that her hump might fly away?'

I was ashamed of what my mother said. I hadn't thought about the hump myself. I'm very fond of Keïra, I walk around with her, it doesn't embarrass me to be her friend.

My mother would repeat: 'You're envious of her hump, you'd like to have one yourself.'

I was cross and that made me upset. If Keïra was hunchbacked it wasn't her fault, it was the farmer's bull who'd hurt her. She was barely two years old. He'd lifted her up on his horns and tossed her to the ground. Her aunt had told me.

I didn't want to have different clothes on every day any more. I wanted to wear the same dress for a long time as Keïra did. I didn't want my things to be washed. My mother was very unhappy about it. We had become like cat and dog according to my father. He gave me a sermon every day.

'What can you do for these poor people? God is looking after them, he never abandons his creatures, he gives them the strength to live and to struggle. You're a child, how can you understand wretchedness and poverty? You just want to annoy your mother. Every feast day I'll give you some money for your friends and you'll say nothing to your mother. It's a secret between the two of us. And promise me not to anger her any more.'

He never says anything to my mother. He must be afraid of her. I'm always the one who's done something stupid, I'm always the one in the wrong. I cried all alone in my room, then I went down to apologize to my mother.

'I'm sorry, Mum, I promise to listen to you, to obey you, to do whatever you want.'

'Listen Lallia. You're not doing any work at school any more, you hang about all day long, you lie to us. Look at you, you're filthy. Where is the red pearl we used to know? What's missing here, why aren't you happy to be with us, with your mother and your father? No stranger can take the place of your parents. You're envious of the misery of those poor creatures.'

I didn't go out for several days. I did my homework, and on Thursdays I learnt cookery. Mum took an interest in me when I was good and I worked. In the evenings she told me stories. Yesterday she told me the one about the river woman who was called a fairy.

One night the men who worked for my grandfather saw something appear in the middle of the river, which they used to cross in order to get back to the farm. The thing was making strange movements under the full moon. They were very frightened and hurried to reach shelter. One of them had heard talk of the river fairy before, but he'd thought that it was just old wives' tales.

The next day they spoke to my grandfather about the apparition. It wasn't a human being or an animal, they said, we didn't have time to look at it closely because it vanished as quickly as it came. It must be a being from the other world.

My grandfather had a good laugh at the innocence of these country folk.

'Tell me, gentlemen, it wasn't by any chance a wolf or a fox which made you run? I have the feeling that your imaginations have been getting the better of you; you've obviously mistaken a jackal for one of the heavenly angels, or was it Ibliss himself?'

Grandpa was greatly amused by this story and the way in which it had been told to him. The men, embarrassed, thought that he might perhaps be right. They forgot about the apparition.

But, during the nights following the story, Grandpa decided to watch the river. He wanted to know what animal it was which had frightened his men. He had in his mind a wolf which he had seen one day when he was coming back from hunting on his blue mare. The young wolf had barred his way. Its courage had surprised him. It stared at him as if it wanted to challenge him with its shining eyes. Grandpa didn't shoot the wolf, which had then even stepped aside to let him pass. He felt a fondness for it.

Grandpa had hidden behind a mound in the hope of seeing the wolf, which presumably came to drink at the river. After a long wait, he saw a bizarre spectacle. A young woman came out of the river quite naked, and, her arms raised, prayed to the moon. Her long hair covered her body almost entirely. He watched her actions for some time, and didn't leave his hiding place until she'd disappeared into the reeds; then he lost sight of her.

He came back the next day. He saw the same sight again. He began to understand the terror of the men who had spoken to him of an apparition. Grandpa wasn't laughing any more. He was asking himself who could that woman be who was dipping, quite naked, into the cold river in the middle of the night. At first he had thought that it must be to do with some love affair, but he didn't see a man at all. He didn't believe in fairies nor in spirits. He waited up some nights more, but in vain. The river fairy didn't return the following nights. Perhaps, he thought, it's because the moon is no longer full.

He didn't speak to anyone about his discovery nor about his night-time vigils on the mound. He went on watching the place on the nights when there was a full moon.

One night when he was getting ready to go home, two shadowy figures attracted his attention. They were crossing the river just opposite his hiding place. They had come from the side where there were houses and were making their way towards the woods. So he decided to follow them, intrigued, but angry at discovering this night life which he'd known nothing of and which must always have been going on on his land.

One of the silhouettes lit a torch. It was an old woman, and Grandpa thought he recognized her. She was carrying a tray under her arm. A young woman was with her, carrying a bag on her shoulder. Grandpa followed them, taking care not to be discovered. He kept at a certain distance.

Now it's obvious, he said to himself, that they're going towards the cemetery. Were they going to visit the dead during the night? Were they going to bury an illegitimate baby that they had killed? Grandpa tried to find the reason which could bring them to this place at such an hour. The two women went into the cemetery, the one putting down her tray, the other her bag. The old woman began to count the graves:

'Is he buried in the eleventh grave of the first row?'

'Yes, Mama, I think so,' replied the young woman, her voice trembling with fear.

It was indeed old Aïcha, Grandpa's maid. He was very fond of her. He used to say: 'She has the courage of the strongest of men and the wit of the cleverest.' But what was she doing with one of her daughters in the cemetery?

The daughter looked terrified. Her mother even gave her a shake, telling her that she must be brave if she wanted to keep her man – she mustn't be like a wet rag. The old woman, her tray close by, began to dig up the corpse. She took out the body in its still white shroud. It must have been the most recently buried, and Grandpa thought of the poor farm-worker who'd been kicked in the stomach by a horse and had died instantly. For a moment he thought that he would intervene, put a stop to it all, his temper was rising. But he changed his mind, curious to see what they were going to do right through to the end. He remained silently hiding behind a tree.

The old woman's gestures were precise. She had obviously dug up corpses before. She herself made two holes in the shroud, and then ordered her daughter, who was whimpering with fear, to pull out the dead man's arms. Then she put the body close to the tray on to which she poured some semolina.

'Come on,' she said sternly, 'stop shaking. Get behind the corpse and hold his back, you can see that I'm having trouble getting him to sit up.'

Old Aïcha recited some lengthy phrases which Grandpa didn't hear very clearly. She had squatted down behind the dead man and was using his fingers, as stiff as pieces of wood, to roll the semolina which was on the tray.

The two women quickly put the corpse back in the tomb, replaced the *chaheds*, poured the semolina into the bag, picked up the tray and scurried off. It was indeed Aïcha, the mother of the stable-boy, and her daughter. But they had forgotten to put back the stone which covered the grave. Grandpa said to himself: 'See how, tomorrow, the country people will spread the rumour that Azraïn, the angel of death, has made the one who's gone suffer for his bad deeds. He even left the stone aside to warn them and put them on their guard.'

Grandpa didn't know what he was going to do. He suspected a link between the river fairy and old Aïcha. Perhaps it was her daughter who went out at night and prayed to the spirits under the moon. He decided to see the river woman again before speaking to Aïcha. A doubt was nagging in his mind. There was something about the fairy which he recognized.

He waited one more night for the full moon, and this time hid in the reeds very close to the place where the woman had appeared. She undressed a few steps away from him, and then slowly went down into the water. A clear beam of moonlight was illuminating her face. Grandpa couldn't believe his eyes. The beautiful river fairy was his own daughter. She was as if possessed. She was leaning forward in the cold water, caressing her breasts and her whole body as she spoke to the moon.

It was Aunt Nadjia, who'd been living with the family for several months. Grandpa had separated her from her husband. He went to fetch her one day against her will. Ever since she had been suffering over the absence of the man she adored. Grandpa was preparing to get her a divorce in order to break the bond which tied him to that family – since he was fighting a courtcase with them over some land.

Then Grandpa told Grandma what was going on. She already knew, she knew how unhappy her daughter was and she too had said nothing about it. Grandpa, angry, mad with rage, took his daughter back to her in-laws and swore never to see her again. Then he decided to do battle with all this monkey business done by women who'd sold themselves to the devil, as he put it. He went to see old Aïcha who had initiated all the local women. He didn't like this witchcraft business, which would end up by poisoning men, especially on his land...

Old Aïcha was in the shed milking cows. Grandpa pretended that he was just passing by. He didn't want to use force. You don't get anything out of these witches by using force, he thought. He preferred the idea of frightening her. He told her about the events in the cemetery as if it were a dream he had had. Old Aïcha began to tremble. She thought that Grandpa was a seer, a saint. She threw herself at his feet and embraced them, asking for his forgiveness. He asked her to interpret his dream, he said that he knew she was reputed to have that gift. The old woman renewed her pleas and her supplications.

'My daughter has been cast out and beaten by her husband, oh master, have pity on us. He tore her baby from her breast and has kept it with him. I'm trying with all my might to return her to her child who, they say, won't stop crying. Master, her milk flows in rivers over her dress. I'm a weak woman, what can I do? O master, be good to us. I know you hate and have forbidden these acts – done by defenceless women. I promise that I'll never turn to witchcraft again, and if my daughter is beaten and cast out, then it's God's will, it's her fate.'

'Get up and explain what all this means.'

'Master, the semolina which you saw in a dream being rolled by the dead man's hands is to go in the couscous that my daughter's husband will eat. Because the semolina has been rolled by a corpse my son-in-law's hands will become as stiff and useless as those of the dead man when he wants to beat my daughter. I confess also that I've killed a white hedgehog. I took out its heart while it was still warm to whiten and soften my son-in-law's heart towards his wife. O master, forgive me, these are women's matters. Forgive, master, I'll never do these things again, if I do, send me away from your lands and I'll go and wander in the woods like a mad thing.'

'Do you know how long the river fairy has been appearing now?'

'O master, since I was born I've heard talk of the fairy.'

'Have you ever seen her?'

'No, master, I've never seen her with my own eyes, but

68

they say that every fifty years the fairy summons the most beautiful of all the local girls and drowns her at the bottom of the river. Perhaps you remember that young girl who was found about fifty years ago, her body floating naked on the surface of the water. It was the Beni-Hammad's daughter, she was supposed to get married a few days before. She was only seventeen.'

'What else do you know about the river fairy?'

'They say that she's as light as the day and looks like the most beautiful woman in the world, that she doesn't wear any clothes and that her hair covers her right down to her toes. She talks to the moon and to the river spirits.'

'Are you sure that you don't know anything else?'

Old Aïcha swore by all the saints, kissing the hem of her master's burnous.

'In future try not to do it again. Tell me what tribe your son-in-law belongs to. In a week at the most your daughter will be back in her own home.'

The old woman thanked him once again and hid behind a cow to wipe away her tears.

After hearing that story I was afraid to go out. For a long time I stayed at the window listening to the noises in the courtyard, thinking that a body or a ghost might be hidden behind the fountain. But no, I was at home, my father hadn't yet gone to sleep, he was trying to get the Egyptian news on the radio. My mother wasn't asleep yet either, and besides the outside door was locked, and all those stories happened a long time ago, before I was born.

The cat knocked something over. I jumped.

'What is it?' said my mother.

'Nothing, the cat frightened me. He knocked something over.'

'You keep on being frightened, Lallia. It's always the same with you. You beg me to tell you stories, and then look what happens. You can't sleep, you wake everyone up. You keep the light on in your bedroom all night long. This must stop Lallia, this really must stop.'

I didn't say anything, Mum was right, it was true that I only liked ghost stories and then afterwards I was scared. It was like when I went to the cemetery on Fridays. I would go with Mum without even thinking about it, I would walk down the paths, look at all the graves, read the names and the ages of the dead people, but in the evening I would shake with fear. Yet I'd be at home in my bed.

I overcame my fear, I braced myself, put on a bold look and went out into the courtyard. I came back and opened my science book for a change. I shall never ask for stories again. I shall never go to the cemetery again. When I hear people talking about the dead I'll block my ears.

Stretched out on the bed, I looked out through the window

into the night. The curtains were drawn apart, I thought that the devil had come up the glass to threaten me. I got up and drew the curtains in front of him. He couldn't see me any more. I bolted the door and fell asleep. In the morning the fabric of the lampshade was singed. The lamp had stayed on for several nights.

My father called me, I wondered what he was going to say.

'Do you know anything about this envelope? I found it crumpled up near the entrance.'

He had been attracted by his own handwriting as he picked up this piece of scrap paper in order to put it in the dustbin.

I didn't know what to say since it was I who had originally taken the envelope, which had been full of money. I'd kept the envelope crumpled up in my schoolbag for a long time and then, yesterday, I must have thrown it down by the entrance without thinking. My mother had said nothing to my father. She knew all about it. I'd betrayed myself with the wretched envelope.

The affair dated back to over a month ago, it was just before Mother's Day. I was at the shop and Djilali took advantage of my being there to go and get his hair done at Miloud, the hairdresser's. I had stayed all on my own. Mother's Day was coming, and I wanted to give a present to the hunchback's mother. I took the envelope from the till. There were several banknotes inside. I bought chains, rings, brooches, scarves, haircombs with coloured stones on them, and perfume. I had wrapped it all up in my bedroom into a number of little packages. My father had bought two presents. One for Fafa and one for me, so that we could give something to my mother. But I wanted to give Aunt Adda a present and I also wanted her children to give her presents. I made a package for each of them except for the boys. I still had some money left which I gave to Keïra.

The school had organized a celebration for the parents in the courtyard. We gave our presents to our mothers in front of the teachers. My mother never came to these women's occasions, and she always made fun of those who did. I asked the little hunchback's mother to come and take the place of

71

mine. Aunt Adda was delighted, she put on her lovely green dress with big flowers on and her yellow and blue scarf which had lots of countries arranged in a map on it – the man in Germany had sent it to me and I'd given it to her.

I'd put on my white dress and my red ballet shoes, with a ribbon around my waist. Aunt Adda sat like the other mothers on a chair under the chestnut trees in the courtyard, with her daughters nearby; but Keïra had hidden with the presents to give her a surprise at the moment when the present giving was announced over the loudspeaker.

On the platform which the school had set up there was a big desk on which the presents had been arranged. The teachers called out the names of the mothers who came up, and each little girl would take her present and give it to her mum, then the mother would go proudly back to her place, and her daughter would wait with the others to sing the Mothers' Day anthem at the end.

When my turn arrived I signalled to the hunchback's mother that she should come up. I went up to the desk and the teacher gave me my package. Keïra's mother got up clumsily, not knowing where to go. She laughed at this herself. I'm a peasant woman, I come from the mountains. And she came forward with exaggerated movements.

She was speaking very loudly, clicking her tongue. She was so happy that I was no longer at all embarrassed because she didn't know how to behave in public. Her daughters pushed her and at last she got to me. All the other women were looking at her, some of them were making fun of her.

'Is that your mother?'

'Yes, Madame.'

I was terrified that the teacher had realized that I was lying. But I had spoken without hesitating, and she didn't say anything. I gave the present to Aunt Adda and gave her a kiss. I was so happy to have a mother there too. Aunt Adda, all emotional, let her veil slip. And then you could see her lovely dress.

Keïra the hunchback and her sisters also gave her their presents and their mother, feeling spoilt, went back to sit down with her packages. She was the proudest woman there.

On the way home, the excitement over, she asked us where we got the money from.

'We saved it up over a long time, bit by bit,' said Keïra.

'We worked with H'nifa at Mme Naguerla's for several days without telling you.'

Aunt Adda had chosen to open her presents at home. But when she unwrapped them she was dumbfounded.

'What on earth made you buy this jewellery? It's junk! Who is the shopkeeper who sold you all that? He's a thief! You shouldn't have wasted your money! This is doll's jewellery, this stuff. Keïra, you're the oldest, you know what's what, what got into you? Did you fall on your hump or something? And the shopkeeper, what a swindler! Selling all these bits of gilt to children! It must be that swine of a Benali.'

I realized then that I'd done something stupid, and Keïra said from behind:

'You see, I warned you that it was the wrong sort of thing to buy, but now it's too late.'

Aunt Adda was really angry.

'Keïra, go quickly with Lallia back to that worthless Benali and ask him to give you your money back for this pile of tin! Tell him that if he doesn't I'll go to the police.'

I refused to go with the hunchback and went home. The next day Aunt Adda came to see my mother. I didn't know where to put myself.

'Excuse me, Madame, but your daughter has given me a present and I've returned it to the shopkeeper. I've come to give you the money back! She might have taken it without saying anything to you. You know we all have children, we know what they're like. Sometimes they have funny ideas.'

I couldn't understand why the hunchback's mother had come to put me in such an awful situation. And that Keïra had confessed everything!

My mother spoke to her in the hall and didn't invite her in. My mother was furious, but she hid her rage completely in front of that poor woman. She remained calm as if it were to do with someone else, not me. She told Aunt Adda to keep the money.

'Lallia does as she wishes with her money. She took it out of her moneybox. You may keep it.'

When the hunchback's mother had gone, she immediately came back to me.

'So you steal money now! And this story about jewellery, what's that about? You haven't touched my things, I should hope?'

I didn't reply, I didn't cry. I was watching my mother get worked up, threaten to lock me in the boxroom for several days without giving me any food. She even wanted to take me away from school. All the better as far as school was concerned. I hadn't wanted to go for quite some time. And if I was to be sent to the nuns I should be quite happy, I wouldn't have to see my parents any more.

A few hours later, my mother took me in her arms and clasped me to her heart. I was so surprised that I was quite suspicious.

'You know that I've said nothing to your father about this business of the jewellery and the stolen money? Why do you do it, Lallia? What don't you have at home? Why do you prefer being with others? Those people are dirty, do you want to catch fleas and infections? I'm always giving you clothes for them, why do you prefer what you steal?'

I didn't reply, scowling and hanging my head.

'Lallia, did you steal that money from the shop till?'

'Yes, it was in an envelope in the till.'

'Do you think that's a good thing to do?'

'No, not at all.'

I had thought that it was all over, and here the questions were beginning all over again.

'So Lallia, are you going to give me an answer? Do you know anything about the money that was in this envelope?'

'Mum knows all about it.'

My father went out and found my mother in the garden. She must have explained everything to him since he never spoke to me about the money again. He hadn't noticed what had happened until he discovered the crumpled envelope.

I got on much better with my mother now. I would go and visit her at her loom, and she taught me how to weave patterns. I went with her when she was invited out.

'Lallia, you haven't seen my silk blouse have you? You know, the green one with the tie.'

I couldn't reply: I'd given that blouse to Aunt Adda. My mother looked everywhere and discovered that lots of other clothes had disappeared. All those clothes had been sold at the market by Keira. I couldn't even get them back. My mother was furious.

'How unlucky can you be! I have an enemy in my own home, my own daughter. I've never done anything to hurt her, but the hunchback's mother, she feels sorry for her and weeps over her fate. Her daughter has found her an idiot to look after her! But what have I done, for God's sake, to deserve this?'

I didn't feel at all upset as I watched her cry. I don't know what it is about me, perhaps I'm really wicked. My mother continued to moan, and I couldn't bear it any longer.

'Stop crying over spilt milk. I don't steal anything any more and I don't give anything to the hunchback any more.'

That evening she started at my father.

'You're so weak, your daughters are just the same! Look at what you've made of Lallia, an idiot. She's like you, she's ready to follow anyone. Now she's stealing from you, that's the result of the fine education you give her. I can't take it any longer, I've had enough of you, of her, and of the lot of you. I'm leaving you all, I'm off.'

My father didn't reply. He let her talk and went to take refuge in his room. He never replied to her taunts. Later, when she'd calmed down, he'd go up to her and comfort her, taking her in his arms and talking to her in a very gentle and slightly mocking tone.

'She's your daughter, do you want me to kill her? What more can I do than you do?'

'Watch over her instead of spending the whole day in the mosque with your muftis telling each other a lot of nonsense.'

'If you like we'll put her in the convent boarding-school

for a while, she'll forget all this nonsense.'

'We'll see.'

I went on doing stupid things. I don't know what got into me. I went to Aunt Adda's, and I spent the whole day with her in the fields. I got tired and sunburnt, my head was spinning and my vision was blurred. I may have got sunstroke. My hands were blackened by the plants which I'd pulled up with Keïra and her mother for supper.

I washed and went up to the terrace, I opened my school bag and got out my work. I spread my books and my exercise books out on the table so that it looked as if I were working. I didn't want to talk or to be with anyone. I put my head in my arms which were resting on my open exercise books and drifted off to sleep. I was woken by my mother's voice.

'Who is it?'

'It's a girl from Lallia's class,' my sister replied. 'She's brought a note from the teacher.'

Blood rushed to my head.

'Come in, dear!'

'Mme Timoléon sent me. She wants to know why Lallia wasn't in school today.'

'Lallia wasn't in school?'

'No, she wasn't there, not this morning nor this afternoon; I said to the teacher that she might be ill.'

'Right! Thank you dear, her father will go and see your teacher tomorrow.'

My mother flew into a rage which left me unmoved. Without a glance, without a pause, she went straight to the table, took my books and threw them from the terrace down into the courtyard, taking good care to tear them first. She vented her anger on my things as if it were me she was tearing apart. I didn't move, I felt so ill, it was as if there was a flashing light in my eyes, squeezing my eyeballs, which were quite hard.

I didn't speak to anyone for a week. I didn't even stay a month with the nuns before my father came to fetch me back. The day I came back I overheard my mother arguing with my father from behind a door.

'Did *they* order you to bring her back from the nuns? She

was beginning to work well again, and at least over there she wasn't seeing the hunchback any more. And here you are bringing her back for mysterious reasons. As if we don't even have the right to educate our children as we like these days! You have to go through them to make even the smallest decision, do you think that's right? Don't you think there's any hypocrisy in your organization? In what ways does the fact that a child is a boarder in a convent school hinder the revolution? The sisters don't force their Christian religion on her in any way. And then there are others like her, Si Mahmoud, the lawyer's, daughters; your colleague, the mouderes's, daughter and this one and that one's daughters.'

'Yes, but I've got to set an example.'

'So, it's you who's preaching all these fine ideas.'

'The gentlemen who you've just mentioned all collaborate more or less with France. As for Si Mahmoud, he's going to take his daughters away too.'

'Well I don't agree with what you're all up to. They aren't satisfied with all the money you give them, the lorry loads of goods that you send into the maquis every week, or do you think that I don't know about all that? It's all very well your not telling me anything, I still know what's going on, I know what you're doing. You all talk about justice when you're being completely unjust yourselves. I know about that too. You threaten and punish those who can't give you any money because they're poor and haven't got anything. You attack wretched people who've got lots of children to support.'

'Saliha, you can't possibly understand, it's not that simple. I know where you get your information from. Those women haven't got their ideas straight either. And then let's not talk about all that. Someone might overhear, the walls have ears.'

I laughed when my father said that. I thought that the wall with ears was me.

'Tell me,' my mother went on, 'all those evenings you're away, those night-time meetings you have in the Jews' cellars, aren't you afraid that you'll find yourself in prison one day, and what will become of the children and me then, do you ever think about that?'

77

'We choose places that they couldn't possibly suspect. That's why those meetings take place in the "Jews' cellars" as you put it.'

I wondered who these people were that my mother was talking about. Perhaps they were the same as the ones who told Yves's parents to leave their farm.

When I asked my father who the bandits were who kill dogs on the farms, he told me never to talk about bandits and never to bring the subject up.

At school we learnt the history of Gaul, of Vercingetorix, of the Franks, the Huns, the Vandals and Charlemagne. And then they told us a bit about the Arabs, who came from no one knows where, and they told us about the battles of Hilab, Sidi Okba and others which I can't remember.

My father told me about the French. They came from no one knows where too. They won a battle and they settled here. There were no French here before. There were certainly no very poor French people. I'd never seen any French people as poor as the hunchback's family, some Jews perhaps, but my father said that they weren't French, they were a bit like us. They were our cousins. There were even some who lived in the black quarter with the Arabs. God hates injustice.

'But then Daddy, why does God let them be rich and take everything?'

'God doesn't *allow* anything, he watches. Our ancestors must have disobeyed God and perhaps they strayed from his path. Today it's us who pay. God never said: sleep and I shall watch over you, toil not and I shall feed you. God said: work and I shall help you. Defend your land in order to merit it! Nothing is owed to you.'

'But then why does grandpa have khamasses and why do lots of tribes work for him?'

'Your grandfather is their brother in blood. He speaks their language, he has the same religion as they do, he shares the same faith. In addition your grandfather is of noble birth, he is a descendant of men of great faith. They are happy to serve him, that's their belief, he's their master, but they're not his slaves, they're his servants. They are proud to serve him.'

78

'And do you agree with it, Dad?'

'My father is also of noble birth. He has lands and tribes who serve him. But my father has disinherited me and I don't see him any more.'

'Why did he disinherit you?'

'Because I don't believe in the same things as he does.'

I looked at Dad's moustache which hid his upper lip, and I promised never to repeat what he'd said. Wearing his indoor *gandoura*, he would make the radio crackle trying to get Radio Cairo. They gave news of our country.

I felt very close to my father, I felt as if I were sharing a secret with him. When he came home from the mosque at about five o'clock, the grey cat would be waiting for him on the little wall under the lime tree. He would appear at the corner of the road like a god, in his black suit, his gold chain protruding from his waistcoat, shining in the sun. I would ask the time in order to have the pleasure of looking at the handsome watch warmed by his body, and I would hold it in my hands for a few moments.

He would bring us back all sorts of things. On the pavement the almond blossom would fall fresh pink and white. The grey and silver tarmac road would gleam in the sun, making stars in my eyes. The cat would throw herself at his feet and would rub against him, gazing up at him. She would talk to him and celebrate his return with loving eyes. He loved that cat. Sometimes she had kittens. My mother would keep the best one and kill the others, drowning them in the pool.

Their eyes would still be closed. They would never have the time to open them. They would move about in the water, their little pink tongues protruding slightly, they would float, and their mother would climb up on the edge of the pool, miaowing. Unable to help them she would climb back down, thinking they might be somewhere else, then she would search everywhere, rubbing against our legs.

'My kittens are in the water, please get them out.'

But it would already be too late, their stomachs were full, they were no longer moving. The one who escaped drowning, because he was white and yellow, miaows, happy to be alone

79

with his mum. He curls up, his mother caresses him and consoles herself by licking him.

'Mum, do cats understand death?'

'No, as soon as their smell has gone, she'll stop looking for them. Anyway, she has that one.'

My mother would send the little kittens to sleep with children's cough medicine before drowning them so that they wouldn't suffer. We used to bury them in a corner of the garden and for a few days the grey cat would go and sniff at their grave.

Fafa went off on holiday to the country, and I stayed with my mother. She was nice to me, and on Thursdays I went to the baths with her. I went with her on the mornings when she went up to the cemetery. A light wind would gently caress my hair and I would watch Mum's veil swell out. When we went along the road canopied by plane trees, their leaves basking in the sun above, we below would be in the shade. The road would be deserted, I'd wear my hat and I'd sing with Mum who taught me an old legend sung by a poet: one day in the desert he had discovered a human skull, he asked it lots of questions in verse. After the poet had finished asking the questions, the skull replied, and told him its story.

We sang the chorus together. When our two voices came together, I felt emotional. I would run happily to gather flowers to give to my mother. She was very slender and straight, she walked majestically with a regular step. I would move several steps away from her so that I could come back towards her and admire her. Her shoulders bare, her face sunny and relaxed, she smiled showing just the tips of her teeth. Soft strands of her shiny hair, black as a raven's wing, would blow up and caress her cheek. She had slanting eyes, and her *sarouel*, slit high on her leg, would be blown up by the wind. Free under her ample transparent veil, which allowed you to guess at the colour of her bodice, she would stretch out her hands and wrists decorated with exquisite rings and bracelets with little carved flowers. She would breath in the perfume of the jasmin branch I'd given her.

That day we were going to the cemetery. We avoided Friday because Mum didn't like the crowd of women who came with their children: they would shout, run along all the paths, climb

81

the trees, pick the fruit which belonged to the dead and crack almonds on the tombstones.

The women would get out biscuits and give them with dry figs to the poor children who came to the cemetery to beg on Fridays and holidays. The cemetery was very large and there was a lot of greenery. The plants grew freely, hiding the old graves which one day would disappear underground. Then a new body would be put on top of the old one. It could be any body since a grave which has disappeared doesn't belong to anyone any longer.

The plot reserved for our family was very big. We'd already had two deaths. A little brother who was Mum's first baby. He had died suddenly one day when he came back from school. He'd said: 'I'm tired' and went to lie down in his room. An hour later, my mother heard a cry. When she went to him he'd stopped breathing. The doctor said it was meningitis. My mother was ill for a long time after she'd lost her child. At that time she was pregnant with me. She would often speak of this little brother, who was very intelligent.

Alongside the little brother was Dad's uncle's grave. He was in the army. In the picture at home he was in uniform. He had a moustache which curved upwards. He had a fine *cheche* and an engraved dagger.

When we arrived at the graves, Mum would greet the dead. I also learned to speak to them.

'Greetings, people from another place. Rest in peace, heavenly countenances!'

And my mother would say to my little brother:

'You, the innocent, chosen by God to be an angel, now paradise is your garden, see that we poor mortals stay in good health and that all evil is kept away from our path and from under our footsteps so that we can bring our remaining children to the age of maturity. Give us the wisdom to stay away from the temptations of sin so that we might join you one day.'

I would climb my little brother's almond tree and speak to him in heaven. I would break off a branch and offer it to Mum as if it were my little brother who was giving it to her.

As I went along I would help her pull up the weeds and my

mother would tell me the family names on the tombs. She would tell me how people died. Mysterious deaths, accidents. Others died in their beds. 'They were the lucky ones,' she would say. I would walk along the paths and stride across the graves without a fear. I would crouch down and watch the comings and goings of the travelling ants and of the little grey things which ran along the stones. They shone like pearls in the sun. They had several thin legs and their rounded backs were striped like a pleated skirt. They were called the creatures of the dead.

My mother would go into the saint's koubba, a very large, whitewashed square building with a dome and a crescent moon. Inside there was a little courtyard, a gallery and some stone benches with blue and white tiles. At the back there was a niche where there were candles and some djaoui burning. An old man sat crosslegged on a sheepskin, the Koran open in his hands. He was the cheikh of the koubba. He lived at the cemetery and watched over the dead. Opposite him would be some children reciting prayers. Their slates were whitened with sansal, the stone which secretes a white substance when it is soaked in water. On their slates there would be prayers, written with the oily ink which the cheikh himself made. They used the stem of thinly cut reeds for pens. These, with their blackened tips, were piled in a wooden box.

Then we would go into the courtyard of the koubba. In the first room to the left there was a vast green coffin mounted on legs and covered with a rug embroidered with holy pictures, its fringe sweeping the ground, and in the centre there was a crescent moon and a star. The coffin had two windows on each side. I used to think that one day a dead man might put his head out of one of them to frighten the people who were carrying him. Or perhaps he would run off.

Near the coffin there were all the tools used at burials. I was terrified of that room and I clung to my mother's veil. The second room was always closed. Its green door kept its secret in. I have never dared ask my mother what was behind it, I was so afraid of finding out.

Inside the *koubba* there was a large airy room with two

83

windows at the back which overlooked the back of the cemetery. In the middle, panels formed a sort of tall wooden chest with an openwork design like embroidery, with two little arched doors where the saint's tomb was. The panels were covered with wide pieces of satin and fringed velvet which women had offered to the saint. On each visit they perfumed them. According to ritual you go around the koubba wiping your face with the cloths and kissing them. You get impregnated with all the perfumes. My mother, however, didn't have the right to make offerings. Her ancestors didn't allow her to go into the tombs of lesser saints.

Sometimes the cheikh's pupils would be called to recite some prayers over the tombs of our dead. We gave them some money and also gave some to the cheikh's wife, so that they would water the plants.

When I played in the war-memorial square, the smells of the cemetery would waft over to me and I would wonder whether the dead weren't calling me.

My dear Lallia,

I think about you a lot, I miss you, I've had enough of being in France. I want to come back to our town. I don't like showing what I'm thinking because I'm shy. I often dream of the day in the barn on the farm, we had fun, it was good, do you remember? Sometimes I burst out laughing all on my own when I think about what happened. My mother has decided to return and wants to leave me here. I don't agree. Don't worry, I'll be back.

> *The cowboy who loves you and who's sad at not being able to go out straight away into the war-memorial square so that he could hold his daisy close.*
>
> *René*

P.S. The post's disrupted so I hope my letter arrives.

I didn't know what to do with that letter. I'd almost forgotten René, I'd stopped thinking about him. I didn't go out into the square any more. It was his fault. If he hadn't gone off, I wouldn't have had all that trouble at school. I would have been happy to go there if I'd known that he wasn't far away, and that he was going to meet me after school. But now I wanted to get away too, to leave that town, which I didn't like. I felt alone, like an orphan.

My mother had gone to a wedding and hadn't taken me with her. I stayed in my room, reading and re-reading René's letter. I kept crying without knowing why. The stork was in her nest, I opened the window and had the idea that she was speaking to me.

'Lallia, there's a quiet spot on the other side of the railway line. If you want to, come and meet me there, when it's the siesta, in the marshes behind the asphodels.'

I wanted to, but I was afraid to go on my own. If René were here, I'd go with him.

'Lallia, it's for you, it's Yves who wants to see you.'

'What does *he* want? I thought I'd told him not to speak to me again.'

'Sorry, Lallia, I've had a letter from René, I'll show it to you if you like.'

'He's written you a letter, so, when's he coming back?'

'His mother's coming next week, but he's not sure that he will be coming back. You know, I think it's because of all that trouble with bandits. They've burnt their farm and all the animals. They've cut their dogs' throats and have told the workers not to work for them. His parents want to leave for good, they're furious because the police haven't been able to stop the bandits.'

'Your farm's not been burnt, has it?'

'No, because my father doesn't work for the government. They're only burning those people's farms.'

'That's not true, I heard the prison warder's daughter talking at school about the Ceccaldis' farm, and they're not in the government, they're working their own land.'

'Well, I don't know. We've had nothing stolen, no killings, and my father still goes to the farm every day.'

That evening my parents were asked to dinner by Yves's parents. It was very hot, we would eat outside under the climbing vine. I didn't know why, but I couldn't stop crying.

'What's wrong Lallia, are you crying?' my mother said with a smile.

'No, I'm not crying. I just got something in my eye from blowing dust away from the edge of the terrace.'

I hated my mother, I hated her. She was always making fun of me.

My father and Yves's father walked up and down the alley talking in low voices. Without seeming to, I was listening, pretending to search through the gravel looking for nice round pebbles to play five stones with. My father was talking about a friend who'd just been arrested and was in prison. He'd been beaten and his moustache had been torn out, each hair was pulled out individually.

My mother hadn't gone to that wedding, she'd lied to me. She'd visited the wife of the man who was in prison. She had five children and didn't know how she was going to feed them. Dad was helping them. Amongst his papers the police had found a card with a green crescent moon and a red star. It was the flag of the club which Dad belonged to.

After dinner, while the grown-ups were talking, the children watered the garden, arguing over the hose and the watering cans. A perfumed breeze drifted over to the parents who were sitting outside on benches around the stone table.

It was after school: I was leaning on a little wall, with a trick pack of cards in my hand, pretending to look into the future. I felt as if I was being watched and so looked up. René was going down the road on his bicycle. He waved at me and went on his way. He hadn't even come to see me, I wondered why he'd written me a letter then. He went by with a wave as if he'd never gone away, as if he'd seen me the day before. He was a liar too, he hated me and I hated him too. It wasn't me who'd burnt his farm. Well, too bad.

Suddenly the bicycle came back and went down the alley. René jumped off and let his bike fall. The wheels went on going round on their own. He opened his arms and held me against him. We stayed like that for a long time, listening to each other's heart beat, feeling our warm bodies.

'René, some really terrible things went through my mind when you went by just now.'

'I did it on purpose, I thought you were going to cry, I'd have liked to kiss your tears away.'

'I'd have gone home to cry, you wouldn't have seen me.'

'Do you want to come for a bike ride?'

'You can't get two on there.'

'Yes you can, you get up on the handlebars, I'll hold you. We'll go to the water tower. Come on.'

René went through the narrow streets of our town. We went past lots and lots of young men in military uniform, dragging their big boots and their passes.

'There are lots of soldiers here now, before there was only one barracks, now there are three.'

'That's no good, you need the "leopards" against the fellaga.'

'Who are the fellaga?'

'They're the bandits who're plundering the countryside, and now even houses in town. Haven't you ever heard your parents talking about them?'

'No, never.'

'Well, they're the ones who robbed us and who cut my dogs' throats.'

'And these soldiers, where do they come from?'

'From all over the place, from France.'

I went home astounded by what René had said to me. I was scared of all that sort of thing. He knew lots of things. I didn't know anything.

'Dad, the bandits they call the fellaga, are they Arabs, like us, or are they French?'

'They're Arabs like us, and they're not bandits.'

'Why are they called the fellaga?'

'It's the French who call them that, because they're against them. They want freedom.'

'But isn't it an Arab word, fellaga? It means thugs, doesn't it?'

'Please, don't talk about these things! Do you talk about this outside with the others?'

'*They* know all about it.'

'Right, well, you're not going out any more. Besides you're not a child any more to go and play outside. Stay at home, you've got things to do here.'

My father was angry, I'd never seen him like that before. I was silent. I thought something serious must have happened. But what?

My father told me off every time he found me in the road. I looked out for him so that I could get home before he got to the square. I was no longer allowed to go out in the alley when he was there. Yves and his sister didn't go out any more either. They stayed in their garden or sometimes came into ours. I didn't see René any more, I didn't even know if he was allowed out. Yves gave me news of him from time to time, they were at the same school.

A woman who lived in the black quarter came to see my mother. My mother sent me off on an errand immediately so that I couldn't hear what she was saying to her. The woman kept referring to the brothers. That was all I could hear.

I didn't know why that part of town was called the black quarter. There were no blacks living there. Perhaps they used to. That part of town was separated from our area by the cattle market and the main street. I should have liked to visit the black quarter, but I was a bit afraid. Over there the boys were badly brought up, and would say rude things to us. It was only Muslims who lived there, and they were all very poor. There were also two or three Jewish families.

In the upper town there were the Catholics and some Muslim families like ours. The other Arabs, and French, lived in different areas. The Muslims and the Catholics in the upper town got on well, they knew each other and some even visited each other. The Muslims were pious and respected the traditions, but they also took part in Catholic festivals because of the children and the school.

I once heard my grandfather talking about the French and the farmers who settled here, but I was too small, I didn't really understand. Grandpa always had trouble with them because they wanted to take his land away from him. They thought that he had a great deal, and he refused to be their caïd. So they took him to court, they wanted to take 'the house of silence', the land he loved best because it belonged to Lalla Smâa, his grandmother. He paid lawyers for years and years. He was often angry with them. 'They'll have to go', he would repeat. I think he hated them.

Fafa knew more than I did, but she was never willing to tell me anything, she thought that I repeated everything. She was happy to help me so that I could play in the square, but as for explaining anything to me, not a chance. She didn't want to.

My parents were becoming very strict about my going out, they said I was too old, but I knew it was because of the soldiers. They'd put up a lot of temporary buildings in the town, kinds of sheds made out of tin. You often saw army lorries driving through the streets.

Even my mother didn't want to go out on her own now. When we went to the baths, Djilali came with us.

When we went to the baths, the hammam, I forgot about all the troubles. About René and the others too. I played at being the married woman. I helped my mother put the nicely pressed clothes into the raffia seppâ, a seppâ lined with pink silk with an oval mirror in the lid. We would take the silver m'hibess, which had long-stemmed flowers carved on it. This was a big jar in which we put all our toiletries. In the m'hibess's various round cups we put soap, henna, ghassoul and the hair-removing cream which my mother made up. My mother made me a very pretty pink fouta out of the same material as hers, slightly transparent and striped with gold thread, and fastened by poppers at the side. I also had kab-kabs like hers. Those were painted wooden mules, held on your foot by a band of red leather, decorated by hand.

I particularly liked Si Nasser's mosaic hammam. When the linen square was hung up at the entrance that meant it was the women's day. Inside the round hammam there was a gallery with cabled columns, which ran round an enclosed courtyard. On the right as you went in there was a little wooden counter, carved in the same pattern as the panels which covered the walls. Old Djoudja, the cashier, sat behind that counter all day long. She looked after the jewellery and the watches which the women left with her.

My mother and I would settle in one of the rooms reserved for certain families. We shared ours with the Khalils. We came on Thursdays and they came on Saturdays. Inside that little room a very high window let in a multicoloured light. The panes were painted green, yellow, red and blue. A wooden couch went round the walls for you to rest on. The walls, which had a mosaic in the shape of stars, shone under the rays which came through the panes. There was a mirror fixed under the window opposite the door, which opened on to the gallery where other women were chatting as they undressed.

You felt good there. No one had the right to come in apart from women and children. Boys over the age of three were not allowed in. Some saleswomen set up their squares next to their suitcases, out of which they would pull piles of things. A real women's souk. The perfumes, the materials, the necklaces and all sorts of things competed one against another. It was a place to relax in.

My mother had covered the couch with a decorated rug which she had woven specially for the hammam. She would put the bath towel over it when we came out so that it didn't get damp. After we'd undressed, we put on our foutas. My mother loosened her black hair which she brushed for a long time. Then we headed for the hot rooms, taking little steps so that we wouldn't slip. Our kab-kabs clacked on the tiles. We crossed the corridor, where there were lots of basins in which icy cold water taps were running, and then arrived at the heavy wooden door, which we pulled – releasing burning steam which would catch us in the face. I shivered and suddenly got goose pimples. I adapted to the new, often very high temperature little by little.

The interior of the hammam was circular too. There was a large room, divided into several recesses, which opened on to an arcaded gallery. In the middle there was a smooth round block of marble as high as an altar, which was known as the 'hammam's navel'. The masseuse would lay the women on it to wash them. A narrow channel went round the hammam's navel like a belt round a waist.

Here too we had our reserved recess and our basin. For in each recess a little semi-circular marble basin was fitted into the wall, out of which hot and cold water spurted as if from a spring. The water flowed constantly, covering the polished floor. I would stretch out on my back, eyes closed, listening to the strange sounds sent back by the echo. I loved the atmosphere of the hammam, it made me think about religious music and singing. When I opened my eyes and saw the glass ceiling, where the daylight mingled with the points of light from the lamps hanging in a corner, I felt as if I were in a church at the bottom of the ocean.

Women, shining with water and sweat, came in and out with things in their hands. One woman was on the navel, being vigorously massaged, her body as limp as if she were dead, her eyes half-closed. The crouching masseuse seemed all concentration, her head bent, her hands tirelessly kneading the flesh.

Another woman, her legs apart, sitting on her crumpled fouta, rubbed her daughter's head, white with foam, her daughter crying: 'You're hurting me, Mum, you're hurting me.' A young girl, muffled up like an Eskimo in her white hooded wrap, made for the door.

In the recess opposite, two very young women, newly married perhaps, were stretched out on their stomachs very close to each other, their chins resting on their folded arms, telling each other secrets. You couldn't hear them, only see their lips moving. Their numerous bracelets clinked on the marble whenever they moved or changed position. The clear water streamed over their naked hips. The noise of silver cups against marble went from recess to recess. I heard snatches of conversation, the voices magnified by the echo. In the silence which reigned for a few brief moments you could hear the music of the water.

One of the recesses at the back was very hot. You could hardly make out the women moving about inside. Thick steam, like hellish smoke, cleared your nose, enveloping you in a strong smell of eucalyptus.

My mother gently washed my hair without hurting me, I had a very sensitive scalp. Then she would put my hair up in braids so that she could give me a rub. She herself would be washed on the hammam's navel, by the Skeleton. That was the masseuse's nickname. The women called her that because she was very thin. Yet she was very strong. It almost hurts when she washes you, my mother told me.

Sometimes I would meet a friend and we would spend hours telling each other stories or playing as we washed one another. The bath lasted all day. When we got tired we would ask the lady who looked after the clothes outside to bring us our wraps. Muffled up from head to toe, my hair under a benikâ, I would go out behind my mother, who walked slowly with her large pink satin shawl, which had white birds painted on it and a long fine fringe which fell onto her shoulders.

My mother rubbed sweet almond oil perfumed with musk into her body, an oil she made up herself. Her face would be pink and her skin smooth like a baby's. Sometimes she would put some on me and I would be shining and soft like her. Like the other women, she had removed all her body hair. Afterwards she would calmly dress after helping me to get dressed. Leaning against the pillar in the gallery, I waited for her, watching a saleswoman laying out chains and earrings for a lady who was inspecting them, crouching opposite her in her wrap.

Suddenly there was loud hammering at the entrance door. We didn't know what was going on. Djoudja-the-cashier got up and went towards the entrance with some difficulty for she was very fat. She returned in a state, her arms raised, shrieking.

'Get dressed quickly, ladies, get dressed quickly, the soldiers are coming.'

'Soldiers? What do they want?'

'Tell them that it's only women in here. You mustn't let them in whatever you do.'

The soldiers were already there, in the courtyard. The women hadn't had the time to get dressed again. They cried out and hid one behind another. The children, quiet up till then, began to bawl. The soldiers, machine guns in their hands, their faces red, their eyes frantic and wild, began to search throughout.

'Bring out the fellaga you're hiding, bring him out.'

I hadn't ever seen these soldiers before, they were the kind René'd told me about. They had berets and uniforms made out of leopard skin.

'So you don't want to bring out your fellouze?'

'But sir, there's no one here!' said poor Djoudja, trembling, her hands clasped.

All the women were gathered in one room and were waiting for the soldiers to go away so that they could finish dressing.

93

'They dared to come into a women's place. What an outrage! They're trying to humiliate our men. Why did I come today?' said one woman, rocking her baby to make him quiet.

'What an unhappy day!'

'This is going to deprive us for ever of the one day out which our husbands still let us have.'

While the women made remarks the soldiers insisted that they'd seen a man come in. There were only three of them, but they'd already turned the hammam upside down. The mattresses were turned over, clothing and shoes thrown into the middle of the courtyard. They didn't put anything back, they were very bad-mannered. I wondered who the fellaga was that they were looking for, perhaps it was a prisoner who'd escaped from the gaol? It had already happened once before. At a wedding. But that time it was the police, besides they hadn't been so rude. And then the women weren't naked.

Old Djoudja was in despair, she lumbered after the three mad wolves. She tried to stop them from going in and surprising the women in the steam rooms who hadn't yet realized what was going on. In French, laced with Arabic, she begged them, swearing that there were only women in the hammam.

The mad wolves finally left without going into the water rooms. Then the women began to exclaim and get indignant.

'Come on,' my mother said to me. 'Let's go quickly. Your father will hear about it and get worried. Look at these women all excited at men catching them with no clothes on! Instead of getting dressed and going, they're standing talking about it.'

On our way out, a lady said to my mother:

'Did you see that? Chief's daughter, did you see what humiliation is like with a Christian face?'

'When you're shamed, you go back home, you don't settle down comfortably to discuss it. They could come back and then what would you do? Go back to your home.'

'You think they'll come back?' said the woman, starting as if she'd just seen them again.

'We're at war, perhaps you've forgotten.'

My father was away from town. He didn't know anything, until my mother told him, about what had happened to us at the baths. I was in a good mood because the evening after we'd been to the hammam Mum didn't work at her loom. She would cover it up and sometimes she'd forget about it for several days. It was her hobby. She loved weaving us beautiful things to wear in the winter. When she worked on it late, sitting for hours behind those white threads which trembled under her fingers, like vermicelli come alive, I would watch her, waiting for the 'little woman' to appear.

I'd been afraid ever since she'd told me the story of a poor woman who used to weave late into the night in order to make a living.

Far out in the country, in a lonely house, there lived a widow. In order to live she would weave burnouses and blankets. She was a good and determined woman, and didn't dare refuse the work she was offered although it was often difficult. She would work all through the week, never leaving her loom. She would stay up till daybreak passing the wool between the threads, which were stretched out like ghostly skeletons, and twanged against her nails dyed by thick coats of henna. Her neighbours kept bringing her wool to weave. She would weave, weave, driving her fingers on. She would only stop when she was dropping with sleep.

One Sunday night, when she was weaving as usual, by the light of an oil lamp in a niche in the wall above her head, she kept dropping off to sleep, waking up with a jump and starting work again – looking at the pile of wool waiting for her like a mountain by her side. She would summon up her courage and start work again. Briefly she saw a little creature pass in front of her loom. She went on, absorbed in her work.

Suddenly the little thing, holding on to the threads, climbed up to eye level. Went back and forth commanding attention. Then the woman saw a little woman, standing no taller than a frog from the spring, dressed up and bejewelled like a queen. The little woman was going up and down along the loom, holding in her hand an animal's tail, plaited like a horse's tail, a horse as tiny as she was. She was at the height of the poor woman's eyes – who was petrified, her eyes staring and her mouth agape. The little woman kept on repeating: 'Sunday wants her revenge, Sunday wants her revenge', without looking at the weaver, who was trying to pray and who wanted to get up and couldn't. The little queen went on rhythmically in a threatening voice: 'Sunday wants her revenge, Sunday wants her revenge.' Her voice got louder and louder, and a cold shower of fear drenched the poor woman's body as she sat listening to her.

In the morning, at daybreak, two old ladies come to fetch their work, found the woman dead, her face blue, in front of her loom.

When my mother was weaving late, I would pull her by the arm and beg her to stop. I wouldn't leave her until she got up and covered up her loom. When it was me who was passing the yarn between the cotton threads I would imagine the little woman no larger than a frog, standing, her hands on her hips, waving her horse-tail whip and saying to me: 'Saturdays it's forbidden. Saturdays it's forbidden.' But as my father wasn't far away and the light wasn't just an oil lamp, I would hold out against the little woman. I felt that she wanted to take me by surprise.

Sometimes she was the little girl's voice which I heard in the television as I turned it on. She must have gone behind and slipped inside. When I opened the drawer in the chest next to the loom, I would do it slowly in order to catch her. But when my parents went out into the garden, I wasn't crazy enough to stay by the loom. I would run and join them.

The television was put next to a window which opened on to the garden. We put chairs opposite it in the fresh air, where we could smell the roses and the mint. We all watched a comic war film with Yves's parents.

It was warm, a lovely summer's night, with stars which seemed to want to share in our happiness they were so low. They sparkled in the dark sky like sequins on my mother's gauze scarf.

On the other side of the gate, they were getting things ready for a dance. They were hanging strings of lights in the trees in the war memorial square. The band were setting up on the steps near the plinth under the soldier, who stood, his weapons raised in one hand, in the other an olive branch. The musicians were tuning up. The soldier on the monument had never been so well lit.

Some soldiers went by with girls on their arms in dresses with puffed-out skirts, their hair in pony-tails or waving over their temples. Their feet, squeezed into white shoes with stiletto heels, tip-tapped along the ground. Their dresses were all light-coloured and sleeveless with low-cut necks, because of the heat.

Everyone was watching the preparations for the dance, to the sound of the accordion which was opening and closing like a caterpillar walking along. Yves, his sister and I took advantage of a moment when our parents were absorbed in the film to slip out into the dusk as far as the gate. From there we could follow the fête much better.

Drunken soldiers, clasping each other by the shoulders, were singing a song about their mothers. You'd think that the idiots were about to fall over. The music sharpened up and the dance began with a waltz. The men rushed towards their partners, pulled them on to the dance floor, and in the same movement, took the first steps of the dance.

The music was loud and the girls showed their legs as they

whirled around. Yves held me and we tried to waltz, he stepped on my toes and we began again having swopped sides. We didn't know how to go about it. We watched the couples and tried to imitate them.

Suddenly there was a noise like a clap of thunder, all the lights in the town went off. We were in darkness and ran shouting to find our parents. We clung to them surprised and worried. The girls at the dance cried out too, the soldiers called to each other, we didn't know what was going on.

Our parents gradually came to their senses and tried to get some light. We children were still upset, clung to them trembling, and followed them about. There was still shouting in the square and, in the darkness, we heard the sound of hobnail boots on the road. Someone brought a candle which made terrifying shadows on the walls. We were told to go home. I held my father's leg, clinging to it so fiercely that he had to walk with a limp. We glimpsed silhouettes, their backs bent, hiding in the alley. A great silence had fallen after the explosion and the shouting. People were surging into the hotel opposite the square. Soldiers with torches were again running in all directions.

Then the town lights came back on again. The town-hall siren sounded three times. The parents, behind the shutters which were now closed despite the heat, were listening to soldiers under the window who were talking about a terrorist attack. The terrified children wouldn't leave their parents, who tried to reassure them without any success since they themselves were so frightened.

Little by little the square cleared and the crowd dispersed. Everyone went home, a child on every arm. They bolted their doors. Yves's father came back to my father and together they mounted guard on the terrace. The army lorries came out like sheep from the barracks and went one behind the other, followed by tanks rolling along on their caterpillar tracks towards the countryside.

I couldn't sleep, the noise of the tanks filled my head and made me imagine that I was being crushed. In the morning my father brought news from the mosque where he'd been to pray as usual. There had indeed been an attack that night on a big bar in the town. Several policemen had died, including even a station officer. Some civilians, passers by, had been wounded, and also a policeman I knew, who directed the traffic in front of the school.

For several days the soldiers made raids in the town and in the countryside. They carried out searches in certain areas and mounted guard throughout the night in front of certain houses. They arrested a lot of people; the soldiers went about in large numbers, ready to shoot. On the radio they discussed our terrorist attack and also lots of others which had taken place in other towns.

A lady came to see my mother; she wasn't happy because, she said, there were innocent people who died in these attacks. She was unfortunate: her husband had to give money otherwise he'd risk being killed.

'We haven't got enough money to live ourselves, and with that, we have to pay, pay. What can we do, we're threatened on every side, in the day the soldiers search us and treat us as fellagas and criminals, and in the evening we have to find or borrow money for the others. Sometimes I think I'll light a big kanoun, let it burn in the room and close everything up. We'll be delivered from our misery while we sleep. When we can't give money we're called traitors and we risk going the same way as the dogs.'

I pretended not to be listening to the conversation, but anyway my mother wasn't watching me. She didn't say anything to me any more when I stayed. She didn't even notice whether I was there or not. She gave the lady some money in front of me, some semolina too and some dried vegetables.

During break a girl called all the other girls in the class together, to show them some photos which she'd cut out of a newspaper which her father had brought home. She showed us the cut-throats. They were the first to have been arrested by the military. They were strange: really small with jet-black hair and eyes not like ours. They didn't look like real men. No one knew where they came from.

'Did your father see them? With his own eyes?'

'Yes, he saw them, when the soldiers got them out of the lorry. They surrounded them and kept them in the sights of the machine guns, they had handcuffs on too. They're no bigger than I am, they have something on their heads, like television aerials. There were a lot of soldiers and only two cut-throats. Even so the soldiers were afraid that they'd escape because they're very strong and highly dangerous. The soldiers were shaking with fear.'

'What were they wearing?'

'They were wearing cachabias with big leather belts over them, with lots of knives. Their feet are very long and their finger nails curve over. I think they're made of steel.'

'My father saw them too. They've got lions' heads. That's why you can hardly see their faces on the photos.'

'Do you think they eat children?'

'They like soldier meat best.'

'Hide the photos, the headmistress is coming.'

'What are you hiding behind your back? Give it to me.'

'Nothing, Madame, nothing, they're my father's photos.'

'Give them to me.'

The headmistress confiscated the photos and forbade us to get together again. She punished the whole class.

'It was Yolande who told. We'll get her when we go home. Right? We'll pull out her hair and tear up her exercise books.'

'Yes, but she'll get her father to come in, he's a prison warder.'

'Are you scared? Get lost, we won't play with you any more.'

'Let's not speak to her.'

At home time, Yolande got a hiding. She got into the lorry which took the prison warders' children back to their houses which were a bit outside the town. Her hair was all undone, and quite a bit of it was left on the pavement. She was crying, her things half-torn, clutched to her chest.

Several girls were sent away from school because of Yolande, also they didn't work hard and made things up.

I passed in front of the boys' school to see if René was there. I wanted to talk to him about the cut-throats that I'd seen in the paper.

'Do you know René?'

'The judge's son?'

'Yes, the one who lives near me.'

'Yes, he's in my class, but he doesn't come to school any more, I think he's in France, why are you looking for him?'

'He lent me a book, I'd like to give it back to him.'

'Keep it, he's rich enough to buy another one.'

'Are you a friend of his? I've never seen you before.'

'I live near the station, the house at the garage. You know, Bentolba's garage, he's my father.'

'You're Khalida Bentolba's brother?'

'Yes, that's right, I'm called Rachid, I know you all right, I see you every day in the memorial square.'

'You don't come by on a bike sometimes do you?'

'Yes, a blue bike, brand new.'

'I remember now.'

'Are you going home? Can I walk along with you?'

'Yes, shall we go by the main road, in front of the chemist's?'

'You're not afraid of your father?'

'I do what I want.'

'You get talked about a lot at the boys' school. One time the bookseller's son wanted to wait for you with the others

102

and beat you up, I was the one who stopped them, they're all afraid of me.'

'Why did they want to beat me? Have I done anything to them?'

'Yes, you only go out with French boys, they say that you're in love with René, the judge's son. His father doesn't like us, he even sent the father of one of our friends to prison. We took revenge on René, we beat him up after school. He was with his gang too. We won, we slaughtered them. Only Boualem and Frichkha, two of our gang, were sent away from school. Salim's father put him in a reformatory, he doesn't get on with his father. Poor Salim, he really suffers from having a traitor for a father. All the others attack him, but I take his side. It's not his fault if his father's a policeman.'

'Do you know Yves? Was he in René's gang?'

'No, Yves's always on his own, he doesn't go around with anyone. He's chicken, a real wet.'

'You're not against him? I can still talk to him?'

'Yves, you can talk to him, but don't tell him anything, he's still one of them. If you're not with us, you're against us.'

'Yes, I'm with you.'

'I've been thinking about you for a long time.'

'Why didn't you write me a letter?'

'The others say a lot of bad things about you. One day they even saw you with René at the water tower. They said he was kissing you on the mouth. I didn't want to believe them, I even had a fight with one of my friends. They wanted to go and see your father to tell on you.'

I dreamt about the cowboy every night. When I told him about my birthday dream he laughed at me. He told me that he didn't remember anything, that he hadn't dreamt at all. I used to think that when you dreamt about someone he knew about the dream, since he was in it too. The cowboy remembered my real birthday party, which was at Dr Maler's before he went to France. In the dream it was a bit different, Dr Maler's house was even more beautiful. The mahogany table in the dining-room had a mirror above it. The table was laid for coffee and cakes.

The cowboy was sitting opposite me, we were alone. While he was slipping under the table to touch my feet, I was looking at my hands in the mirror and making rabbit shapes with my fingers. When I lent over the table, my face swelled in size. We were playing at making the doubled up glasses and spoons talk to each other. In the reflection the spoon and its double were transformed into a beautiful woman who was going towards the knife, which the cowboy was holding upright. It was the reflection of a gentleman. He made him walk towards the spoon who was ahead of him.

'Good morning, madame.'

'Good morning, monsieur, how are you?'

'I'm well, thank you, how are your children?'

'I don't have any children, I don't have a husband. My husband died in Indochina you see. Otherwise I wouldn't be here talking to you.'

'I haven't had time to get married yet. The people who live over there, in Indochina, have slanting eyes and flat noses, their faces are as round as biscuits. I fought over there, it's a muddy land and I had mud up to my neck. Now, I shine like a silver knife, and I look at my double in the mirror. One day, in Indochina, I hid in the mud so that I wouldn't be killed by the bombardment. There were soldiers running after me, those people run amazingly fast. I went into a house, the first one I came across. There was a woman, a native, she hid me under a blanket as I was, covered in mud. Afterwards she washed me, and I wanted to marry her, she was beautiful, if you knew how beautiful she was, that Indochinese woman! She was gentle and had a small, tender voice.'

'As for me, Mr Knife, I don't know Indochina, there's no point in talking to me about the women there, I don't understand a thing. Anyway, I shouldn't like to go there, there's always a war on.'

'I had to go, they made me, it was my military service, I didn't sign up, you know, I'd never do that. But I'm not married.'

'Perhaps you want to seduce me, Mr Knife. Farewell, I don't want to see you any more, you're impolite. I'm an honest woman, from a good family. If you bar my way, I shall tell the policeman who's over there, that glass standing on its long flat foot.'

The day of my real birthday, there were several of us, I'd invited Yves, his sister, Rida and the cowboy. We'd eaten little buttered biscuits with fish roe in the shape of tiny black balls. It was a bit like the lead shot which we got out of birds when my cousins brought them down with their guns. Dr Maler told me it was caviar. It was very good, it comes from cold countries.

In my dream the caviar was the heads of shiny black ants who were crawling about. The cowboy and I ate some as if it were real living caviar. You have to eat a lot of it when it's cold to warm you up. In the countries where you get it, they eat tons and tons.

One day, I saw snowy mountains with streaks of blue light all around them. There were men in a sort of low pushchair, like the ones babies have. They looked like the seals you see in pictures. They were dressed like them. They had dogs, as big as wolves with thick white hair, who were pulling them along as horses pull a cart. They had little hills made of snow with holes inside. My father told me that that was where they slept, that was their house. These strange people were called Eskimos. The name was written on the picture which I found in the box of chocolates which the man in Germany sent me. I wondered how these men escaped catching cold when they lived in houses made of snow. They even lit fires inside.

In my dream, after the cowboy and I had eaten the birthday cake, we suddenly found ourselves, as if by the wave of a magic wand, in Dr Maler's bedroom. A bedroom, all in blue, with two double beds and a garden in the middle full of flowers the same colour as the blue you use to rinse sheets so that they won't be too white. They were spotted like ladybirds and their petals were soft as silk.

On each side of the beds there were wall lamps with seven branches apiece, which each held a candle. Everything was reflected in the mirror on the wall. A dark woman, viewed from the back, leaning to one side, one hand placed close to her hip, was sitting in a frame hanging between the two beds. Perhaps it was Dr Maler's fiancée. A heavy wool carpet covered the mosaic tiles. Daylight came in through the window, which opened on to a balcony where veils, as light as the wings of ant brides, billowed out. It made me think of a woman who was expecting a baby.

I took off my sandals and slipped my feet into some ladies' slippers which were on the bedside rug. I felt that I was a real woman and I began to grow. I was wearing an open wrap like my mother's, with swansdown around the neck. I moved around slowly, swinging my hips with every step, the belt which was undone kept slipping down around my legs. I was leaning on the balcony rail, watching children playing tag in the square. They were chasing each other, tapping each other on the shoulder, and then crying:

'You're had!'

'René, don't you think that's a stupid game?' I said to him.

'Do you think our game's any better? Well, I'm bored, I've had enough of watching you showing off as if you were a woman,' he replied.

The cowboy dragged me out on the terrace and I lost a slipper en route, he'd gone mad, he took the hose and sprinkled me from head to foot, then he left me there, drenched, and went off to play with the dog by the kennel. I was furious, my make-up was running down my face and I was smudging it all trying to wipe myself. My lipstick was smeared round my lips as if I'd eaten blackberries. I went back in, cross, swinging my shoulders. The cowboy had really angered me.

I went down from the first floor and went into the surgery which was on the ground floor on the right. The cowboy was there, I don't know how he did it. I looked at him in amazement. He was sitting behind Dr Maler's big desk as if he'd been there forever. There were two skeletons, a man and a woman, standing behind him making faces. The cowboy looked up. He had the face of Dr Maler. He held out the skull which was on one corner of the desk. He wanted to frighten me. But I'm only afraid of real corpses, those with flesh.

The medicine chest was closed. Behind the sliding glass doors of the bookcase, the books were squeezed one against the other, telling each other stories. I couldn't hear them, they hid their secrets from children.

The cowboy was buried in the large armchair with a wide back, which was bigger than he was. You could see the patterns stitched on the leather. He was wearing Dr Maler's glasses, which annoyed me.

'Stop rummaging in Dr Maler's things!'

'He's not your father.'

'Stop it, or I'll leave.'

The cowboy took Dr Maler's pad and gave me a prescription form which he'd scribbled something on. I crumpled it up and went out into the road.

I was blinded by the sun and my head ached, I woke up. I was in bed, and I saw in the mirror the white bolster stretched out behind me like a corpse. I jumped out of bed terrified. I couldn't even glimpse a sheet any more without thinking about the dead. Every time I went into my mother's bedroom when it was her siesta, it was as if I was discovering her for the first time. I would pull the sheet away.

'Don't cover yourself with that any more, I hate sheets, they scare me.'

Outside thick fog was covering the countryside. You couldn't even see the soldier on the memorial. I tried, however, to make him out in the middle, and I saw him climb down the marble steps, with his bronze jacket and his legs swaddled like a new-born baby's. He came towards the alley, enveloped in mist, getting a little larger with every step, surrounded by a silence broken at regular intervals by the thudding of his iron boots. He became very tall, outstretching the roof-tops.

Little by little the town disappeared, there were no more roofs, no more houses, no more walls, and no more trees. Just a vast square and empty roads. The soldier walked straight ahead. His arms were raised, just as they were when he was on the plinth of the memorial, his moustache curved up to the protruding cheekbones of his face, as closed as a box. He came towards me, I was alone with him in the fog. He stopped, looked down, looked at me as if I were an ant at his feet, and his mouth opened slowly like a machine. He was going to speak.

'Lallia.'

It was Rachid who was calling me, I recognized his voice and came out of my daydream. He'd come to fetch me, as he did every day, to walk to school with me. The fog was slowly lifting, and I went down to meet him before my mother noticed.

School was beginning to be disrupted, the teachers weren't bothered with us any more, they always took the side of the French girls against us, even when they were in the wrong. They passed all the exams. I gave my first draft to Annie and she copied it out. She passed and I failed.

During break people formed into clans, and the teachers encouraged us to keep apart. I was often away, and nobody noticed. I'd met a girl called Zineb. She lived in the black quarter and had never been to school. She taught me things I never knew before.

Boys played ball in the narrow streets where Zineb lived. They would make the ball themselves with rags and old newspapers tied together with string. We hugged the walls so that we wouldn't disturb them and wouldn't get hit by the ball. The little ones, barefoot and ragged, cried in front of the half-open doors of low white-washed houses. Women, standing in the doorways, shouted from one house to another. An old lady, slippers on her feet and a towel on her head, returned the sieve which she'd borrowed from a neighbour at the corner of the street. Dark grocers' shops stank of paraffin and rancid olive oil. These shops sold everything. Materials, semolina, coal and lemonade. Date boxes were filled with bunches of fresh mint. The zinc counters were black. There was often no electricity or water in the houses. The children would fetch water from the local well. The grown-ups had to lower their heads to go through the ill-fitting doors into the houses. The walls were covered with phrases written in henna, coal or chalk: We shall overcome – Down with the French – Death to the *fellagas* – Keep Algeria French.

Zineb explained to me that the soldiers had come round the houses, smashing things up, trying to find out who'd written the slogans. But no one knew. They beat the boys who were playing ball so that they'd confess, but it wasn't them. Yet the village was very merry, with a carnival atmosphere. The little girls sitting on the ground with empty cans in their hands, beat on them like a drum. While others danced and sang, clicking their fingers. Others, also in rags, jostled each other at the wells to fill their buckets. They would bring them back, losing half the water on the way. The buckets were too heavy for their arms. One mother hit her little girl who came back with her bucket empty. Sheets, drying in the wind, flapped, making shadows on the road.

We went into a courtyard because we heard the sound of weeping. The children were playing with the rows of shoes in front of the door to the room where the cries were coming from. The bigger ones were leaning against the wall, watching their mothers in tears. Two women mourners were at the head of a body lying in the middle of the room, covered with a white sheet. The room was packed full of women, handkerchiefs in their hands, brushing away the flies that were drinking their tears. When the mourners had finished the text in which they were describing the life of the dead man, the other women took over from them, wailing in unison.

I cried too, I couldn't hold back the sorrow which was choking me. Zineb looked at me and tried to calm me down. She told me the story of the man who was lying there. He was a prisoner who'd died under torture. She'd found out from an old woman.

Zineb took me out and I stopped crying, I felt a bit better. We went past the butcher's where the flies were buzzing around the sides of meat displayed on the table in front of the shop. I thought that these were the same flies I'd seen a moment ago flying around the dead man, and I felt sick. An axe was planted in the block used for breaking up the bones. A girl with an old black scarf round her head sat next to a straw basket selling biscuits, calling: 'Hot galettes, hot galettes.' Nearby, a little boy, perhaps her brother, was playing with a piece of chalk next to a tin can in which chickpeas were soaking. Two donkeys laden with rubbish, went by, pulled along by two old men. Some chickens flew up squawking above the donkeys. There were some children with bloody feet and shaven heads; they were covered in sores where uncaring flies would land and feast. One old woman, bent double under a load of wood, was complaining without looking up as she struggled on her way. Another, on her doorstep, was offering to trade her poor bits of jewellery. Couscous, rolled for the winter, was drying on sheets spread over large raffia mats held down by stones. A young girl turned the grains over from time to time and then went back to her pile of rags for making dolls, which she did by crossing two sticks one over the other and then dressing them. A group of boys played five stones in front of the Moorish café where the mats were laid out waiting for customers. There were only two old men sipping tea and having a leisurely chat. Another old woman, squatting in front of a *kanoun*, flapped a piece of cardboard over some coals to make the embers catch light. At the bottom of the road a man was grilling spicey sausages which children bought one at a time. They hid while they ate their steaming-hot sausages which dripped with grease. The others, who didn't have the money to buy a sausage, pressed forward with a corner of bread to dip in the drippings which fell onto the table.

Blinding smoke got in our eyes and made them water. We left the street and went into the square which housed the local mosque with its dirty walls. Some old men were coming down the steps, holding on to the door – like children learning to walk – and finally putting on their shoes. Opposite, the school. An old building with high walls on which the white-wash was peeling off in sections letting the naked brickwork show through. The broken panes had been replaced with pieces of card.

Zineb's house was on some waste ground where old cars got dumped. That's where she would go to play. I would bring her some vegetables from home and then come back to play at having dinner with her. She would light the fire, a real one, and do the cooking. She'd made a pot, a couscous steamer and some plates out of clay. She taught me how to make things out of mud, and I made piles of little men.

This is where Zineb would come when her mother went off to work all day for some French people. She would lock the door and leave her daughter out in the road.

I used to bring Zineb money from my money-box so that she'd let me play with her. One day we went together in a lorry to a wedding. We, the women and children, were all piled in the back. We sang and whooped during the journey. We went to fetch the bride from a shanty town.

I stayed with Zineb that night and completely forgot about my parents. When I got back they were very worried, my father had called the police. My dad didn't speak to me any more, he was so angry with me he didn't even tell me off. For my part, I didn't want to go to school any more. Whenever I went out it was to meet Zineb in the black quarter. When there was trouble at home, I would wait till it blew over, and then go back.

One day I gave Zineb one of my mother's bracelets. My mother was furious and I got scared. So I took refuge at a neighbour's, a Jewish woman, who told me I was wrong. She

111

had a long talk with my father and he let me stay with her for a while.

Zineb had a boyfriend at the barracks, a soldier who never came out. They thought he was crazy. He was always locked up because he refused to go out on exercises with the others. He told Zineb that he didn't want to learn how to kill. So he would be punished. He told Zineb everything, it was through him that they knew when there'd be a raid on the town.

I went with Zineb to Faïza's, the madwoman of the black quarter. She didn't have a house, she slept in the tin hut in the cattle market. Her husband was mad too, and went barefoot through the streets. He always wore a white gandoura and had a stick in his hand. He would proclaim that 'there will be war and rivers of blood will flow, brother will make war on brother, men will abandon their homes, the Foreigner will depart, the poor will become rich, and the rich will know poverty'.

'You'll get some shoes then, and perhaps even a house,' said a passer-by to him, smiling.

Faïza, the mad woman, was beautiful, I'd never seen her before. I knew her husband. He was always running about town in the train of some school children who would poke fun at him. Women were always amazed at Faïza's elegance. When she fell out with her mad husband, she would spend the night with old widow women. She would make herself up and go out into the streets without a veil.

'She's the one who helps Zineb's mother make clothes for the brothers.'

Zineb took out of the fireplace a roll of material which her mother had hidden so that the soldiers wouldn't find it. It was thick canvas, green like the forest leaves.

'It's a secret, you mustn't talk about it, not even to your parents.'

'I don't like my parents.'

'You're right, they're not very nice to you.'

'They don't know that I see you, otherwise I'd never get out. They think I'm at school.'

'If you like, I'll take you to see the brothers, you can com-

112

plain about your parents, and they'll speak to them. They're against the French school.'

'They take the side of the children?'

'I know them, they don't like people with money. My brother's at djebel too, he's one of the brothers. He tells us everything.'

One day she took me with her into the capital.

'The brothers say that it's less dangerous when it's children who do certain errands.'

We took the red coach; a man collected money to pay for our seats. We went to a fat lady's house, in the casbah. Zineb gave her a package. She didn't know what was in it, perhaps money. It was in the evening, and we were given a good welcome. We had dinner at the lady's house, on a terrace overlooking the sea. I was terrified when I thought about my parents. Zineb comforted me and promised to get the brothers to intercede for me with my father.

The next morning the fat lady's son went with us to the road. The cars went by very quickly; he pretended to be trying to hitch a lift. A black car stopped, a clandestine taxi. The driver said a few hurried words to him. The car set off and the driver didn't speak to us once during the entire journey. On the way there were road blocks, and the car was thoroughly searched. We'd been told not to speak French and to pretend that we didn't understand it. It was very difficult.

We came back covered in dust and our faces black. At home my mother was sick with worry. No one spoke to me. My father seemed to know what was going on, he was very tired and very sad.

I did what I pleased now, and I stopped eating with my parents. Zineb gave me a letter to take to the soldier, locked up in the barracks, telling me it was a love letter. I didn't believe her. When I got to the barracks, I went up to the gate and waited for the soldier who was called Claude. I was carrying a basket of eggs, as if I were selling them. It was Zineb's mother who'd got the basket ready, which was why I hadn't believed in the love letter, but I hadn't asked any questions.

When Claude arrived he kept looking all around, he was

113

very nervous. He dug into the basket and took the letter, then told me not to come back. They were getting suspicious at the barracks, and they were watching him. I never saw Claude again after that morning. They say he was killed.

I was now very well known in the black quarter. I was the one who wrote letters for all the women. They treated me with great respect as if I were grown up. I wrote to their sons, their brothers and their husbands. I gave them news about their families, their neighbours, and I told them about any arrests. I never put an address, I didn't know where all the letters went.

One day we had an important errand to do. We had to give another letter to the level-crossing keeper. We decided to go across the railway bridge and along the rails to the station. The bridge was very high, and Zineb wanted to climb up the stone wall to get to it. I followed her, but by the side which wasn't fully built, hanging on to the bushes which covered the embankment.

We were enjoying frightening each other, when we heard the train whistle. It was arriving at full speed; in a flash a cry mingled with the train's whistle. Zineb had slipped and crashed down to the ground. I climbed down, shaking and panic-stricken. A man left his donkey and crouched down by the body. He tried to listen to Zineb's heart.

'Run and fetch someone. She's still living.'

I ran to the corner of the road to the military post. There was a soldier there, I told him about the accident and, a few moments later, I came back in an army ambulance. On the way I remembered the letter which Zineb had on her. I was frightened and pressed my lips tightly together. They won't let me get near her. Zineb was motionless and silent, she was lying on the ground as if she were dead. The soldiers got down and picked up her body.

'Do you know her family?'

'She's my sister.'

They let me get up in the back with her and I tried to think of a way of getting the letter back but, horrified by the state Zineb was in, I didn't dare get near her. Zineb was wrapped

114

in a khaki blanket, lying on the thick canvas stretcher. I closed my eyes in despair and dug my nails into the palms of my hands. I tried to guess what might be in the letter. I had no idea what to do. When the ambulance got to the hospital I stuck close to the stretcher. I followed the nurses, clinging to their sleeves.

'Monsieur, I'd like to get something from my sister's dress.'

'Wait here, I can't let you go into the treatment room.'

I was frightened, I was mad with fear, I squirmed about like a worm. The nurse came out again, I asked him once more.

'Wait, I tell you.'

'Monsieur, I'll have to tell you, it's a letter from the brothers, the French might find it on her, I don't know what's in it.'

The nurse was an Arab, and I thought I could try telling him the truth, it was a risk I had to take. The nurse looked at me with a worried expression, he'd gone as white as a sheet.

'*Please*, Monsieur, give me that letter, it's very important.'

'Right, stay here, I'll go and look in the emergency room.'

He closed the door behind him and I stayed there in the corridor, pacing up and down. The women who went by asked me what I was waiting for, and if I was with the girl who'd had an accident. I couldn't stop thinking about the letter and about Zineb. I don't know why, but the letter seemed more important than anything else to me at that moment. I thought that they'd throw my father in prison and things like that. I felt sick and kept sighing.

I fixed my gaze on the door leading to the emergency room, waiting for the slightest movement. The nurse came out and beckoned. In the toilets he hastily passed me the crumpled bloodstained letter; it was still sealed. I was so pleased that I sobbed for joy. I hid the letter in my top, and ran after the nurse.

'How is my sister, Monsieur?'

'She won't die, she's got several broken bones, but it's not too serious. Are you really her sister?'

'No, I said that so that I could come with her.'

'You must go and tell her family. She might be going to be sent somewhere else.'

I set off to go and tell Zineb's mother, but she was already there. She was climbing up the hospital steps, her face anguished and her veil open over her apron. She had heard about the accident at work. I don't know who had told her. She had been to the bridge first of all, she'd been told that Zineb was there. She thought she was dead. She was howling and tearing at her face. I wanted to go to her, but she pushed me away.

She didn't see anyone around her. I went back to the waiting room and sat down on a bench. I cried and cried all alone in a corner. I thought that perhaps everything which had happened was my fault. On top of that I hadn't been hurt at all, not even bruised. Poor Zineb had borne the full brunt. What if the nurse had lied to me, and she was already dead? I came out in goose pimples at the idea, I got up and went nervously out of the room. Zineb's mother was stopping everyone in a white coat who went by, and asking for news. They made her sit down. A nurse explained to her that her daughter wasn't dead, but that she couldn't tell her exactly how badly she was hurt, she was in the operating theatre, and they were going to operate at any minute. Her mother groaned.

'She may be a cripple for the rest of her life.'

Then she began to cry again even more loudly. I was opposite her on the bench when I sat down again. I didn't dare look at her, I held my tears back, and I clutched the letter to me, covered with Zineb's blood. I bent double, with my head on my knees, and began to doze off. Someone came and tapped me on the shoulder.

'Is this the one? Is this your daughter?'

I looked up, my father was there, smiling to see that I was still alive. He took me into his arms, I was astounded that he wasn't telling me off. I wept as he held me, and that helped me to feel better. Despite my unhappiness, I hadn't dared cry too much in front of Zineb's mother. I wanted to show the letter to my father, but he'd gone to find out how Zineb was.

'She's safe, you'll soon be able to see her. They're going to take her to another hospital, where she'll be better cared for. Don't worry, salamate.'

116

That's the way in which my father reassured my friend's mother.

The next day, Zineb was taken to another town. At home it was peaceful once more. The accident was never spoken of again. I was looked after because of my nightmares. In my dreams I saw the cowboy instead of Zineb falling from the top of the bridge and crashing into the ground. I would wake up screaming, and they'd give me some medicine so that I'd go back to sleep.

I went back to school, and promised not to misbehave any more. In a book I found some dried leaves which the cowboy had given me. He'd written: 'Daisy, I love you and send you a kiss.' I put it all into a metal box, which I hid away. *I want to forget René.*

After school I went to look for Rachid. He was going to see the body of one of his friends who'd just died, he'd been drowned while playing with some other boys who, like him, hadn't been to school that day. They'd played at soldiers and fellagas. As he was an Arab, he'd been the fellaga. People were saying that the drowning hadn't been an accident. When he was taken out of the water you could see the marks of the stones which the others had thrown at him before they ran off. His mother was out of her mind with grief, he was her only child. Rachid and I went into the room where the drowned boy was laid out. His body was swollen and covered in red and blue marks.

I'd had enough of all these deaths. Why were they dogging me? I left the shack and went home. At home one of the khamasses from the farm was explaining to my mother that Grandpa had gone up to the maquis, taking all his horses with him. He had organized his own group because he didn't agree with some of the others. They had dug an underground store in the mountains, where they were hoarding various goods, arms and medicines. Grandpa went home to the farm late every night. All the men went with him. They were only at home in the evenings. Only women and young children were left to look after the land.

My mother decided to go and visit. She found everything changed. The orchards were abandoned, soldiers had set up camps all over the place to keep a watch on the area. They had burnt Grandpa's forest down. The French settlers were leaving their farms. The soldiers were raping and pillaging; mothers were marrying their daughters off to anyone available in an attempt to protect them.

Every day, people would talk about deaths and arrests. People would disappear and you'd never hear of them again. Relations between the French and the Arabs were becoming strained. They were hardly speaking to each other any more; grown-ups avoided each other. Children would hide away in order to see each other. Yves's parents and my parents still said hello to each other, and sometimes exchanged a few words. Yves's father wasn't seen in too bad a light by the Arabs, but nevertheless my father avoided him. At school there was no one, half the children were away, and the teachers were always off sick.

I didn't see René any more. He'd left for good. I think he'd moved house. One of the last times that I caught sight of him was in winter. It was snowing, I was on my way to school. The big lorry was clearing up, throwing the snow into a pile at the edge of the road, so that the pavements, cut off from the road by a wall of snow, were like dark corridors. It was a day of raids and searches. I was made to open my school bag on a doorstep and my things were brutally scattered all over the place. The soldiers let me go in the end because the cowboy saw me and rushed over to me, to help me pick my things up. We didn't speak. He took my hand for a moment and then we parted. The soldiers were stopping all the passers-by. People, in a panic, were hurrying to get home.

The last time that I saw René was the morning that I found the butcher in the church square. At home everyone was asleep. I had gone out to fetch some milk, but I'd made a mistake about the time. It was much earlier than I'd thought. The streets were empty, even of soldiers. I went on into the sleeping town, with the feeling that I was being watched, spied upon. The dairy shop was on the other side of the church square. It was closed, and I didn't want to wait till it opened. I was scared of being all on my own, like that, in the town which seemed as if it were dead. I retraced my steps, looking all around me

119

uneasily. I wondered what was going on. The main café was closed too, although it was already daylight.

I was about to cross the square when a body lying on the ground caught my eye. I went up, slightly hesitant. The man lying there was dead, his skull was open just above his forehead. Blood mingled with white stuff which I couldn't bring myself to name. The body lying there was the butcher who I knew well. I'd seen him the day before in the same clothes. His apron spattered with animal blood was now splashed with his own. His curly hair was full of dust as if he'd been dragged there, his eyes were open with a look of astonishment. His arms were thrown to either side, like those of a puppet whose strings had been cut. The palms were turned up to the sky.

I stayed still, stuck to the spot without taking it in, without a sound, without a gesture, as if I were part of the horror. Little by little people arrived, talking in low voices, some asking questions with their lips barely moving. I felt as if I were at the bottom of a well. No one had noticed I was there. I was transformed into an invisible statue for an hour, maybe more. The crowd increased in size, some left, others arrived, a sort of silent ceremony. Someone suddenly shook me by the arm. Someone brought me out of my absent state. I turned round: the cowboy, a prayer-book in his hand, was obviously heading for church. He took me away from the crowd and asked me why I wasn't responding to his signs.

I didn't respond to the questions he was asking me then either. I was thinking about what I'd seen. I gazed at him, indifferent to him and to everything else. Suddenly René left me and ran like a mad thing. Rachid and another boy ran past me like the wind, in an unbelievable rage. They wanted to catch the cowboy to beat him, to take revenge for everything.

I went back towards home. A jeep with over-excited soldiers arrived and drove round the square. An officer was shouting into a megaphone: 'This body is an example to the populace. This is what is waiting for any one of you who collaborates in any way with the *fellagas*.'

I went back to bed, without saying anything to anyone. I had a temperature all day. My father asked me questions, I didn't reply to him either. They were worried about me. I was shivering and very cold. The following day I started having nightmares again. I refused to go out at that time. I didn't want to go to school at all.

But one afternoon, my head ablaze under the torrid siesta sun, I went over to where the cowboy lived. The white gate was closed and the rose petals all split for lack of water. The white-painted chairs with a pattern of holes in the seats were upturned on the round table without a sun shade. The wisteria with its purple and white clusters, rusted in places, was hanging like a weeping willow. René wasn't there any more. He will never be there again. I went to the old disused factory where we used to meet. I called him at the top of my voice. The empty building sent his name back to me.

I went back, distraught, playing hopscotch on the rails of the railway line, hoping for an accident. I got home with my hair frazzled and my face feverish. I took the hose from the courtyard and, while the others were having their siesta, I sprinkled myself with water, fully-clothed. Then I went up to dry off on the terrace. I stretched out on the tiles. I had a mad longing to shout out. I didn't want to think about the cowboy any more, he was one of the enemy, a son of the others.

I became quite mad. I thought that the birds were talking to me, and I talked back to them. Lying on my stomach, my chin in my hands, I told them stories. They flew across the sky with piercing cries and I didn't feel all alone any more.

The smell of coffee enticed me into the courtyard where my parents were. I heard the regular sound of coffee spoons against the china saucers, it was four o'clock, time for tea and coffee. They were drinking and eating cakes soaked in the best honey which my grandparents sent every season. My father had just got back from the mosque, as he did every day at the same time.

When he'd finished my father would go off again on business. At that very moment, as if she'd been waiting for it, Safia, the errand girl, would arrive. She came every morning to do my mother's shopping for her. She went from family to family all day long. For the ones she'd collect the children from school, for the others she did the shopping. She always

121

came at tea time with the news of the day and the gossip from the town.

Safia's laugh, which I heard from a distance, annoyed me. I went down the steps and arrived in front of the meida laid for tea at the moment when she was telling the story of the young woman whose throat was cut by the brothers on the other side of the railway line. She had been walking with a French soldier, people said that she was in love with him. Yet she'd been warned of the risk she was running, the people in the town had pointed it out to her. The two of them had been laid out close together and the knife had cut across their two throats. Now they were well and truly united. The brothers had forbidden anyone to bury them.

'But what on earth made her fall in love with a French boy, and a soldier on top of that, was she mad or what?'

And Safia kept repeating:

'It was a death wish, it was her fate.'

I dipped my cake in my tea. I was tired. I wanted to leave, to go far away, where I wouldn't hear about such things any more. If I could only die and go to join my little brother. Perhaps he was better off there, in paradise.

Deaths, nothing but deaths. There was another terrorist attack. At the greengrocer's, he was a traitor too. Some children were killed. Tough luck on them, they only had to buy their vegetables somewhere else. They had been forbidden to go into that shop. And the old dustman, I was very fond of him, he always had a kind word for me when he went past. I shan't see that old man again, with his rubbish cart and his white horse. His throat was cut, he was found in a stream on the other side of the railway line. His son had signed up as a *harki*. If the father hadn't approved then the son would never have signed up. That's the way it was, you had to set an example for the rest. They tied his feet and his hands. He was stretched out like an *Aïd* lamb, and the knife did its work.

I tried to imagine these men going to their deaths, dragged there by their brothers in misfortune. The ones were heroes and had every right on their side, the others were traitors whose only hope of dignity lay in finding their deaths just. Yet I had difficulty in understanding how a man could lean over another man and look him in the eye before cutting his throat. What were they like, these men? I imagined them big, with monstrous faces and eyes which flashed fire. They couldn't be like my father, or even like the men I saw in the street. Sometimes I would stare at a passer-by, saying to myself: 'Could *he* cut someone's throat?'

What does a man think about when he's trussed up and stretched out to have his throat cut? I even saw a man with his ear cut off. Yes, they cut the ears off lesser traitors, and the noses off cowards. Greater traitors got their throats cut.

The soldiers used sub-machine guns, and did even more horrible things. But I was more disturbed by the thought of cutting someone's throat. I don't know if it was because they did it to their brothers as much as to the others, or whether it was the weapon itself. I was told that it was because they didn't have any other weapons, and that they had to fight and defend themselves, and that when they cut someone's throat they didn't make any noise. So the army didn't pick them up.

But all these explanations didn't stop me from having nightmares. A man stretched over another man's lap, his blood the same as that which flowed in the other's veins. From then on the way the *Aïd* lambs were killed seemed monstrous to me. I couldn't bear it any longer. Seeing the animal tied up and the knife go quickly across... I couldn't stop myself thinking about the men.

When I went out I avoided people. I didn't want to see all those murderous soldiers. All those civilians who perhaps, in the night, took on the role of cut-throats. As I walked an image would force itself upon me: I'd see an enormous shroud going before me. It would be rolling along, and I wouldn't be able to look up from it. I'd be transfixed, my heart pounding. Suddenly I'd find my strength, and I'd leap over the shroud, which held me back. Then I'd run, I'd run like a mad thing, as far as the main street.

The nightmares went on. I'd see the dead come out of their graves and encircle me. They'd be as straight as poles, with no arms nor heads, like bolsters. They'd slide towards me. I'd scream, but no one would hear. I wouldn't be able to run and the dead would gain ground. I'd wake up in a cold sweat, shakily put the light on, but my fear wouldn't go away. I'd look at the things around me in my bedroom:

'Why do these things exist? What if they started talking? Perhaps they do speak. Only I can't hear them.' Then I'd see the chair laugh, the mirror look at me and send back an image crumpled with fear, like another person who'd ask me questions. Who is she? I'd get up. I'd go out, give myself a shake, but every night brought a new fear, and the questions would begin again. Why these deaths?

I used to get down on my knees and pray, facing Mecca.

'O God, my only friend, you who know me, you who know

124

everything, show yourself in a little way, just a little way, to me. I'm afraid, help me, tell me that you do exist, that you will come to us one day, that you are there, that you are protecting me. I'm afraid, very afraid. Give me a sign as you did when you showed yourself at that woman's who had some freedom fighters at her house, and the army tanks, tipped off by a traitor, arrived, and you turned all the freedom fighters into sheep.'

I waited, and the Good Lord didn't show himself, he didn't give me a sign. I remained all alone with my fear. And the more I asked myself questions, the more frightened I became. God stayed silent. I wondered if he really existed. Houses frightened me, stones piled one on top of the other with roofs above, shelters in which men were hiding. Cars, little tin cans which drove along with men bent double inside. And trains which went by. Where were they going to, all these men?

I used to put my head under the tap, and I'd stay under the icy water to chase away the ideas which came to me, and scared me so much. And I would say: 'God exists, God exists, forgive me, my God, my friend, my beloved, I believe in you and honour you.'

II

Very early one morning, the curfew barely lifted, I jumped on a train and travelled sitting on the grey mail-bags. The war was at its height. The Organization de l'Armée Secrète was massacring the people. I didn't even know where I wanted to go, I was driven by deep-seated rebellion, I wanted to be free, free to think, free to act – which I couldn't be in my family. My parents thought I was dead, killed by the OAS. I couldn't get in touch for a week. I looked for an aunt of mine who lived in Algiers, but she'd moved.

A raid took me by surprise. I ran towards the casbah. The casbah with its little cut-throat side-streets, where you met so many friendly faces that you felt safe; with its dark shops belonging to men who worked on copper or for the revolution; its doors opening on to little courtyards illuminated by small squares of light. I took refuge in a passage chosen at random. At that time people were often scattered, far from home. It was commonplace to be in a strange house when there was a raid or a manhunt on. Checks were no longer possible. 'Passes' and 'visit permits' were no longer essential. The Algerian family I descended upon didn't ask me any questions. I was one of them. I knew a girl, a militant, from the casbah. Where I came from, where I was going to, it really didn't matter. In wartime you come out of nowhere and you're going nowhere. You take refuge, you hide, you fight.

Women came out of the dark holes, which were daubed with whitewash tinted methylene blue, and which served as bedrooms, dining-rooms and kitchens all in one. They met on the terraces which were a brilliant white, softened a little by the blue of the sky. At night, on the same terraces, they would utter piercing wails which came from the pits of their stomachs and spread out over all the city. These laments chilled my blood.

During a demonstration the paras came into the casbah. They shot at the men who were running away. The women sang over the bodies of their husbands fallen in the narrow stairways. They called to each other, their wails multiplying in each alley as they gathered up their dead. One woman, carrying her mutilated child whose lifeless body had just been brought to her, climbed up the steps as if in a trance, chanting the revolutionary anthem. As she advanced other women and children joined her. That day all the men found in the lower kasbah were herded together.

I too joined with the women and the children in the battle which followed that demonstration. I threw glass bottles from the terrace on to the soldiers' helmeted heads in the hope of seeing one of them fall under the shards of my bottle.

Peace returned momentarily but never lasted long. After a week I escaped from the kasbah siege. I settled in at my aunt's, who I finally found in an area which was slightly better protected. Then I could at last write to my father.

Dear Dad,

I'm writing you this letter since I've never really been able to talk to you as I would have liked. I'm not a little girl any more. Anyway, when you and my mother decided that I should be married, you must have considered that I was a woman, and therefore capable of living away from home. It wasn't only for my protection that you offered me that rich southerner as a husband. You said: 'A girl who marries takes on a great responsibility.' I didn't want that responsibility. I preferred something else. I escaped as if I were a prisoner, it's true, without a word. I didn't want to hurt you, it wasn't that I was running away from you, I wanted to choose my own life. I wanted to be free, I felt that I was capable of being free. Besides, I didn't have any choice. It was freedom or the marriage that you were suggesting to me.

My dear Papa, I'd like to reassure you, I'm not on the street. For the moment I don't want to tell you where I am. Try to be understanding as I count on you more than on Mum, I can hear her from here: 'She's chosen the street, well, I don't want to hear another word about it. I shall behave as if she were dead.'

She has repeated to me often enough: 'Why were you spared that day when the black Citroen went through the square, with its windows down, and machine guns blasting at the children playing quietly in the square? I'd have wept for you for a few days but today you would be dead and buried and my worries and anxieties would be buried with you.'

I don't hold it against her, I know she suffers a lot because of me and that she often says things which she doesn't mean. You should know that it's not because of that either that I left... I have my future too, and it's not necessarily the one you've mapped out for me. A girl needs freedom too and can fight like a boy.

Try to forgive me, Dad, and ask Mum to forgive me. Tell her that I haven't forgotten that expression and that I believe in it too in my own way: 'Paradise lies under the soles of your parents' feet.'

Your daughter

A few months later I learnt of my father's death. I jumped into a taxi and the same day was back in my home town. I didn't notice the route, I was deep in memories throughout the entire journey, which lasted about two hours. I looked back over all the scenes that included my father.

He came to fetch me one day from my grandmother's, where Mum had sent me to make me think things over after an incident I was involved in at school. It was one of those little things which grew out of all proportion because of the tension between the Arab pupils and their teachers. I must once again have 'shown a lack of respect' for the headmistress, who could hardly see me any more without flying into a rage unworthy of a woman addressing an eleven-year-old girl. It was open warfare between her and me. She would turn red and then blue, her chin would wobble as if I represented everything which she most detested in the world, as if I were, solo, responsible for the entire existence of an awkward and undesirable race.

I'd never been on a train before that day. I was delighted to encounter that magical machine which still has a strange effect on me, far stranger than that of any other form of transport like planes for instance. Trains, for me, mean freedom. My father was reading his newspaper in the compartment and I was looking out of the window at the countryside rushing by like pictures in a film. The stations which we went through all looked alike, and each time we went through a new one I thought it was the same one. The closed gates, the men waiting for the train to go by so that they could cross, the terrified mule which pulled at its cart, wanting to turn round, bucking as if it might knock everything over... Then the train would shake itself again and set off whistling, leaving the station master on the platform already getting prepared to take off his cap and roll up the red flag which he'd been waving just a few minutes before. The train would spit out its steam like an open stove, and the puffs of smoke little by little rise up into the sky.

It was dark when we got into our town. The train woke the little station up for a few minutes. A silhouette waved a lamp in an irregular, wobbly movement. It was the station master who'd just got out of bed. He was in pyjamas and dressing gown. Two passengers pushed open the red and white door with their luggage and then disappeared. On the platform a soldier was hugging an old lady.

My mother was waiting for us near the entrance to our house, in the alley. She was worried about my father, he already had that sickness from which he would never recover. It made him live in a dreadful state of solitude. I didn't believe in this illness. I used to think of all the reasons which could have provoked this thing which had been gnawing at him for several years. I thought that his sickness derived from some painful secret which he was obliged to keep to himself. The silence wasn't caused by the sickness, but the sickness by the silence.

I saw again that scene which had taken place two years before. A group of maquisards who were getting ready to attack some barracks had come to our house to wait until

132

nightfall. We'd covered the terrace with rugs for dinner. The freedom-fighters – there were six of them – were pressing round the pool to wash their hands before coming up on to the terrace. One of those men in green got out a huge knife: the blade was covered in dried blood. He asked my father to clean it. I saw my father in the kitchen holding on to the walls so that he wouldn't fall over. The next day he couldn't get up. He had a high fever.

My father loathed weapons. He preferred books. He was a natural pacifist such as I've never known. But in the situation that his people were in, the danger that his children lived in, his problem about taking up arms suddenly took on a different meaning for him. Weakness? Fear? Impotence, as the brothers would say? He was faced with what you call an affair of conscience, a drama which plunged him into a crisis from which he would not come out alive. He died a fortnight before the ceasefire. He would have been so happy to know that Algeria was finally free, happy to leave his children alive and with as much hope as is still possible. There you are.

I remembered one evening when his sickness was visible in his hollow face, in his body weakened by attacks which seized him from time to time and lasted several days. He was in his armchair near the door, taking the air. A postman came up and handed him a telegram. I saw my father crying like a child, the telegram in his hand. As he looked at me he said: 'He was my son, I was the one who brought him up, they've killed him, they've murdered him.'

He was speaking of the uncle who had taken the place of the son he never had, and who had just been killed at the age of twenty-eight.

When the taxi dropped me in the alley, my father had just been moved to his new home. In fact I'd crossed the path of the funeral train, but I'd turned away from the long procession. I hadn't thought of my father. Perhaps I didn't really believe that he was dead. Another funeral train, you saw them every day. It was a sight which was so familiar to me. I thought that they'd wait for me before they buried him. I would never have thought my mother capable of doing such a thing. I'd sent a

133

telegram which she hadn't received because the post was disturbed. It was raining. My mother explained to me that they'd decided to bury him before the grave filled up with water. She'd tried to make the men wait, but it was no good. She was hoping that I'd come. I was the only one not to be there.

My mother and my sister had watched over him for several nights. He had been unable to speak. They saw his eyes close and felt the last breath of air which he breathed out. Hearing them talk to me about him, I lost all sense of reason, I didn't believe them any more, I was sure that they were hiding him under a bed. I searched all the rooms, under all the beds, in cupboards, wardrobes, nothing could comfort me. I was torn apart. I didn't know what I was doing. I threw myself on his bed and wept. I hugged the bolster, talking to it as if it were my father's body. Saying to my mother who was weeping silently, leaning against the wall and looking at me:

'Why did you do that to me, why?'

She never replied.

In the night I went to the cemetery and tried to dig him up. They followed me and brought me home as if I were a lunatic.

Several days later, the tears and accusations finally gave way to silence and contemplation. I had calmed down. I regretted what I had said to my mother. I was beginning to understand her sorrow. I admired the way in which she coped with it.

I thought back to the day when a man had come from the farm to announce my grandfather's death. He was bare-headed and barefoot. His throat had been cut. Some men had arrived in the middle of the night and had rudely awakened him. He was sleeping in his bed for the first time in a long while. They made him go out in the dark. Near the river, his severed head must have rolled into the water. We never really knew why or by whom my grandfather was killed.

I saw my mother get to her feet and say to the man: 'You may go.' Then she moved her hand away from her cheek and went to the pool. She bent over the fountain and filled her palms with water. She stayed there for a long time like that with her face in her hands. I watched her without daring to go near. I loved my grandfather so dearly. I wanted to go up to my mother, take on a little of her suffering, come into her heart. When she stood up straight she was no longer the same. How does she suffer? I wondered. And in what way is she suffering again today? I feel all the more sad because I can't know her pain, I don't suffer as she does, I can't wash my face in the pool and then stand up without a tear. My way is to weep, howl, shout and accuse.

I wandered aimlessly round the house: I went upstairs, I went down, I went out into the garden, without being able to escape from the painful memories which wouldn't leave me. I locked myself in my room in the middle of the day and drew the curtains. I spent hours lying stretched out on my back, staring at the lamp.

Outside, old and young alike were shouting patriotic songs, standing on the roofs of coaches which were driving slowly past. In all the streets and on all the pavements, people were dancing, drunk with joy, their stomachs bare, sweat pouring off them. Some, their *derboukas* fastened on their belts, beat out mad rhythms as they advanced. A man threw himself off the top of a block of flats for joy. It was Independence.

The nights were open once more, there was no curfew. Children migrated from village to village, throughout the country the entire population was celebrating victory.

How I should have liked to laugh, to shout my joy from the roofs of the blue coaches. How I should have loved to put on my best clothes and go off to see people to share my happiness too. But neither my mother nor my sister nor I could think of it. My father had been dead for a little while, yet his absence had just hit us, as if, during the first days, despite the pain, we didn't believe it. That day the house seemed empty, empty. The very walls called out his absence.

We were free at last. They say that freedom is priceless. But I couldn't manage to be really happy, the price seemed too high to me. In our house there were only women left. Not one of the men in our family had survived the war. Women and young children. And we were already beginning to experience the difficulty of being women.

One day, mother decided to open up the wardrobe where

135

my father's clothes were kept, and to distribute them to the beggars who came round the house in vast numbers every day. As I was taking out his still fragrant garments I recognized the embroidered waistcoat he was wearing when he was arrested.

It was hot that day, very hot, in the height of summer, a stifling summer, such a heat that you could fry an egg on the pavement. We found it hard to breathe. Soldiers had invaded the shops, the bars and the mosque like a plague of locusts. They were piling all the men into lorries which were heading for no one knew where. Behind the half-closed doors the women were shaking their heads and spoke without moving their lips.

'Where are they taking you? Which one of you will ever come back?'

The children kept tugging at the hem of their robes so that they'd be carried. They wanted to see what it was like.

I ran towards the mosque. I broke the curfew like you break your fast at Lent, it had just been called by the town-hall siren. My father was at the mosque. I had no sensation in my feet, it was as if they were flying over the ground. At home the door was locked, my mother had hidden the key so that I wouldn't get out. I had jumped from the terrace, without shoes or hat. A large number of lorries were parked not far from the mosque. A child told me that none of them had left yet.

I looked for a face, I searched the crowd, I was ready for anything. I would not turn back. I would brave all the soldiers. The tank over there didn't frighten me. I slipped under the raised guns. My father had just jumped over the barrier, he was climbing into the lorry, clinging on to pull himself up. He tried to smile, he'd seen me, he wanted to reassure me, he gestured to me to go back to the house. But I stayed and I followed him.

The soldiers were pushing the men, some fell and got up again. Children watched their fathers get up into the lorries. They looked at each other questioningly, their pockets full of stones. I felt grown up, I wanted to strike. The soldiers tried to chase us away, we dug our feet into the ground, we didn't speak, we didn't move. My father's lorry had started up, I didn't know what to do. I picked up a stone. I threw it. The children watched me crying. Then the lorry slowed down, I ran, I caught it up. I caught hold of the bumper, a soldier hit my fingers with his rifle, but I didn't let go. The lorry went in front of our house. There was no one outside. I would die with my father, too bad, no one would know. I could already see the men lined up next to the holes in the ground, blindfolded. The soldiers would fire and they would fall down. I wouldn't close my eyes, I would hold on to my father's leg and fall next to him into the hole.

The lorry arrived at the barracks, close to the cemetery, on the outskirts of town. A soldier gave me a violent push. I got up, they'd already closed the gate. I climbed up along the barbed wire to try and see my father.

The sun beat down. I couldn't see very clearly. I closed my eyes and blood rushed to my head. The men were lined up against the wall at the back of the camp, their hands on their heads. I watched out for the slightest movement or sign from someone. I sat down on the ground and refreshed myself by weeping. I swallowed my tears, bitter as oleander tea. I didn't know what use to make of my heart, my feet or my head. What if I spoke to the soldier who was standing over there in his box? Like a picture on a box of toys. I spoke to him and he didn't reply. He pretended not to see me.

I was going back to my place beside the barbed wire when I saw a jeep coming out of the camp. M. Tessier, Yves's dad, was inside, he recognized me. I threw myself into his arms.

'Dad's in there, they're going to kill him.'

M. Tessier comforted me, he'd been picked up in the raid too by mistake. They were going to release my father. M. Tessier spoke to the soldier and followed him inside the camp. They came back, the two of them together. My father had caught the sun, his nose was all red. He was a bit dejected, but his eyes were shining. I think he'd been frightened. He hugged me to him. We went back home on foot with M. Tessier.

Each day found me on the scent, like an animal.

I spent hours leaning on the terrace wall watching the other side of the square. It had rained the night before, the pavements were still wet and a slight breeze was drying the branches. The leaves fluttered in the air before falling in a pile in a corner of the garden, under the remains of the fig tree. It was a gentle breeze. The gate was closed. The stream was no more than a ditch of dirty water. Some stray leaves were still playing at being sailing boats. On the road opposite the children were heading for school. Their satchels were brand new. Their overalls still a bit stiff. They hurried towards the beginning of the school year.

What if I hadn't grown up? What if all that were only a nightmare and I was still going to lessons and there had never been anything but new terms and holidays?

The schoolchildren went into the yard and began to make friends. The older boys were pleased to see each other again. They wandered up and down, their hands in the pockets of their short trousers. The girls, in pleated red-checked skirts, their socks pulled up, jumped up and down on the spot. They were happy. The little ones wept in the arms of the red-lipped teachers, who were dressed in blue or green suits with little collars, their hair held up by invisible combs or in very high buns. Then the pupils got in a line, the bell had rung.

A boy on the other side of the alley looked up at the terrace. Perhaps it was the cowboy, the boy I used to love. He must be grown up now. Then I remembered... Yves going, and his family. Everyone cried that day. No one was ashamed or held themselves back. We didn't know how to get rid of all the unhappiness we felt. They left the alley and crossed the stream.

138

We never heard of them again.

The boy on the pavement was still looking at me. I didn't recognize him, perhaps he was new. What if it were the cowboy? He crossed the road, went past the chemist's, he must be sad. In the school yard the boys were playing ball and making a din. He was alone in a corner. He opened his satchel, got out an exercise book. He was going to write to me.

Daisy,

I'm at school, waiting for the end of the class. The others are talking about their holidays and what heroes they've been. While I look at the barred window like a prisoner waiting to be let out. I see you with your chin in your hands and your eyes still as if you were waiting. The hours of lessons are never ending and I'm bored. So, do you know what I do? I sharpen pencils, watching the lacy crown which comes out of the pencil sharpener, the lead getting thinner – and I go on till it breaks and then I start again.

I should like those bits of spaghetti, those alphabet letters to mark on the exercise books this absence which is part of me. I'm waiting for the bell to ring. I'm almost happy to be able to escape for a moment. In the yard that bush is still there that you know so well, I suck the sugary nectar from its little red flowers. I make wishes like I did before, I still collect petals like a child. I write 'I love you' on one of them and then hide everything in the big books in the library.

Yesterday I dreamed that I was travelling in a train. I should like to tell you my dream. I remember it as if it were real. In the dream I was big, as if I were a man.

There were no seats anywhere. No free compartments. So I leant on the window, like you do on the terrace wall. It was fine weather, the beginning of summer. I saw a woman at the end of the corridor. She was wearing a white suit of light material and green sandals. She went past me without seeing me, and I thought I recognized her from behind. Her hair had a wild smell which I knew.

I ran through the corridor to catch her up and pushed open several heavy doors between the carriages. The corridor got longer and longer. I became smaller with every step that I took.

And, at the end of the train, I was a little kid who was lost. I was crying as I looked for the compartment where my mother was. A guard took me back and he even lent me his cap. The train whistled in a station... It was my alarm clock ringing, time for school.

You don't go to school any more. You've changed, yet we're the same age. Is it true you're getting married? You don't go out to play in the square any more. There's barbed wire in the park. The swing is broken, no one can go on it any more. I push the piece of rope where the seat is still hanging and it catches on a branch.

I don't like it this side of the wall. On Thursdays, I trail over towards your house. The windows are open but the curtains don't move. As if there wasn't anyone behind the glass. On the way to school I turn round thinking you'll appear, I look down, count the paving stones and bump into posts, which hurts but doesn't wake me up. I'm still waiting for the end of the lesson.

Today I feel old, I'm looking at the corner of the table. There, close to the hole where there used to be a china ink-pot, a heart with two initials is carved. They're not ours. Perhaps our hearts pierced with arrows, cut into that tree during the holidays, will survive the foresters. I'm going to leave, you're going to get married, I don't know where, you won't wear dresses with full sleeves any more, you won't plait your hair any more, and you won't fasten the ends of your plaits with blue slides. I shan't be able to undo your ribbons to make you angry.

You dress like a woman. You leave your hair loose. What does that mean? Don't you want me any more? I feel so small.

The red brick where we used to put our letters has disappeared. You won't be marrying one of the three brothers. Why did you tell me that story about Loundja, Sheherazade's granddaughter? She lived in a palace full of blue light, she was imprisoned by her father, a terrible ogre...

I wanted to be the prince who saved Loundja, I wanted to travel across the world, braving lions and savage beasts. For days and days I'd cross raging torrents, humid nights streaming

140

with scorpions, and finally I'd arrive in the land of the secret tree, where the red earth is always bathed in afternoon sunshine. I too would find the dwarf apple tree which spreads out its branches like a parasol. And like the prince I would grow sleepy and the magic apple would make me see your palace.

Like Loundja in her tower, you'd be locked up and you'd be searching through your hair to find the first white one. The bird would come, like the canary, to bring you news. You too would hear galloping and you'd see dust rising up into the sky and the bird would say to you:

'Don't be afraid, little princess, it's the horse of the prince who is coming to set you free.'

And you'd reply:

'I recognize that gallop, it's my angry father, he's coming to devour me.'

'For seven days and seven nights you haven't eaten and you haven't slept. You never rest any more. Your lips are cracking under the salt from your tears, your eyes are red, your hair tangled by your fingers hunting for the silver thread which hasn't shone as yet. You must get ready. Your prince will come.

I hear him, he's getting closer.'

'Oh! my pretty canary, it's the neighing of the ogre's black horse, coming to trample me. The trials are too hard and my prince has given way... Look, look, little canary, search through my untidy hair, pull out the white hair at the root, for if it sees the light of day, I'll be eaten. Part the black threads one by one and hide nothing from me. Tell me, little bird, how old am I today?'

'Get up princess, get ready to receive your prince. He mustn't see you in despair, with rings around your eyes, he who has braved so many monsters and travelled such a long way. Don't get used to your misery, your lips are made to smile, your eyes to shine. The ogre won't come if you refuse to doubt.'

The canary searches the princess's thick hair. Then, suddenly, the sun disappears. The little bird moves aside and finds his wings again. He hides away in a corner, shivering under

141

his feathers. The magic apple has rolled from the prince's hands and he is retracing his steps. He is galloping, galloping, then falls with his exhausted horse, clutching the apple in his hand.

A cloud of dust rises in front of the palace. The princess goes down a never-ending staircase. On the last step a snake bars her way. The horses draw near.

The princess hoists up her clothing then jumps over the snake which bites her in mid flight. She falls, pale, her face like white paper. The prince opens his eyes, his horse was eating the magic apple. He jumps to his feet like a madman. He is close to the palace. He rushes inside. Loundja was there, stretched out on the ground, the bird on her body.

The prince hears the distant sound of neighing. It's the ogre, Loundja's father, who is drawing near. The prince carries Loundja off on his saddle and the canary follows them. When Loundja opens her eyes the prince is spitting out the poisoned blood which he had sucked from above her ankle.

'Lallia, come and have tea! Why do you spend hours leaning on the wall like that? What is there to see in that street where no one goes by?'

My mother and my sister had tea as they did before. My sister had become a real woman. She dressed in pink silk. Since she got married, my sister didn't talk to me much any more. Mum and she were always together as they were when my father was ill. I didn't know what bound them together, I had the feeling that they spoke a language which I didn't understand. I felt so different, so alone. No one took any notice of me any more.

I followed them sometimes from room to room, they would speak about women's things, what to wear, jewellery. They looked at themselves in the mirror and saw that they looked beautiful. When I looked in the mirror I considered myself ugly and stupid, badly dressed. They went ahead of me. My sister sent me to fetch something from her room. I went into that magnificent room, where necklaces were scattered near her wrap carelessly draped on the carpet. They'd forgotten my father, they'd forgotten him!

'Come down, Lallia! Come and have a cup of tea with us.'

How happy our house was, the fountain flowed calmly, and someone had put a raffia basket of rose and jasmin petals on the meïda. The cakes were soaked in a honey as clear as teardrops. I looked at my mother's fingers which seemed to speak through their gestures. It was at that time that my father used to come back from the mosque. He was very fond of that moment in the day. Nothing would ever have prevented him from being there. My mother and my sister laughed and their laughter made me into a stranger. I wasn't there, I was thinking about my father.

The war memorial square had changed; I couldn't understand it. The soldier wasn't there any more. Had he become a ghost? Or had the boys from the town thrown him to the bottom of the pond one evening? The tiles which had covered the square were completely broken up. All the tanks which had passed through, spilling off the road, had destroyed the design. There were no more flowers. Slimane, the man in blue canvas trousers and battered old straw hat, had disappeared too. You didn't see him any more with his long red hosepipe attached to the park fountains so that he could water the trees in the square.

The steps I used to trot down had become a mass of pebbles, there was no distinction between the square and the road. The circles of moisture which used to sustain the trees had now become circles of cracked and trodden earth. The trees had become sticks. I looked for the precise spot where the memorial used to be. It seemed to me that it was there. I'd already forgotten what the soldier was made out of. Stone? Bronze? And the colour? Dark green? Chocolate iron?

All the girls from my class had married, some had had children. The lime tree had been cut down to let light into Dr Maler's old bedroom. His whole house was being turned into offices. The gate had rusted, only part of it was left. Books, tons of books, burned in the garden. Despite the risk of getting burnt, children would attempt to pull some out of the flames. Dr Maler's library had been emptied so that a property service could be set up. The wind would pick up fragments of pages from the burnt books which drifted by the piles of damp rubbish, tomato seeds and onion peelings which children, come from no one knew where, piled up by the door.

The cattle-market had become waste ground. For the last

few months it had served as a rubbish-tip for the barracks which had been erected at the side. The market fountain where the animals used to drink was now no more than stone ruins, where stagnant rain water mingled with the urine of the boys roaming about looking for sardine cans thrown out by the soldiers. The OAS captain's house which had opened up on to the market was replaced by a wall. They all bricked up their doors when they left.

The roads seemed to me to be narrower, you'd think they weren't the same. The shadows of the trees weren't the same. The siesta sunlight didn't attract me any more and I'd forgotten what winter was like. People's faces said nothing to me, they were all closed and at the same time so feeble. The terrible wind which wrapped my skirt round my legs didn't blow any more either.

No more children under the town walls. No more siren. Four o'clock passed by unnoticed. The shoemender from the square had become a cyclist. And the synagogue had become a shelter for swallows and stray cats. In the church the windows were broken and spiders spun their webs everywhere. The big hotel bar was used as lodgings for the many families who'd come in from the country, families who'd been left without a home because of the bombing. A big flowery canvas sheet had been fixed up at the entrance in lieu of a door. When someone came out, the curious passer-by could see the campbeds and mattresses in the lounge and around the bar.

At night I got woken up by nightmares. So I would go down and sit in the corridor near the door. I would see myself with my hands attached to my feet by wire, thrown into a grey courtyard, my eyes looking up at the stars. Or again, I would see clothing being ripped on my little girl's body which was being held over a charcoal fire on which they'd thrown coarse salt. Or that nightmare when my mother in a rage would throw a heavy object at me from behind. The blow would take me by surprise, it didn't hurt, but when I touched my head my finger would slide into a hole, blood would come into my mouth and I'd swallow it. In the pitch dark room, where I'd been shut up for two days without eating, my mother, woken

145

up by her own nightmares, would come and see me several times saying:

'You smell bad, you smell like a sheep's head, like a boar, like unclean meat.'

Crouching down, my head resting on my knees which dug into my stomach, the nightmare would return. My mother, helped by my sister, took down my pants and was rubbing me with hot pimento, dried for the winter and then soaked in water so that it was unbearably strong. She would rub the wet pimento on my lips and then leave me like a chicken whose head had been cut off. I would dance about in the courtyard, my legs apart, howling with pain. In my bedroom the mirror would show me my lips swollen and red as blood.

Yet another dream. That night, when everyone was asleep, the door squeaked as I went out to see if the soldier from the war memorial came back when it was dark. On my return my mother had taken a knife made red hot in the fire and, helped by my sister, she lifted up my dress. With rapid strokes the red blade went up and down. I lost all sense of where I was, words were twisted in my mouth and I was shrieking: 'Stop that child from crying'. I don't know what death is any more, it seems that it's only for others. If I don't die like that in my nightmares, I shall never die. I was talking out loud, reciting poems. I jumped to my feet, but couldn't see my belly; it was hurting me.

Another time a doctor opened my legs to see if I was still a virgin. I was lying stretched out on the grass talking to a boy of my own age, in between two lessons at school. A black car arrived. Two women got out, with bare faces, looking distraught. They were crying 'Rape'. The little boy got up like a thief and ran off into the fields. I was taken in as a witch. The women consulted each other. They didn't know how to recognize a virgin. So they called the doctor.

And during a night of mourning, a few days after my father's death: I was alone, reading in my bedroom. A head rolled out from under the green sheets against my foot, it went up, up towards me, towards my face. It was my father's head. Just before it arrived at the edge of the sheet, I jumped out of bed and went out into the night. I didn't know anyone in the town, I had to find someone. I knocked on a door. A woman let me in. I didn't want to see that head.

And again, that memory which won't go away: my father who was sick, very sick, he couldn't hide his sickness any longer. He was close to the door, leaning back in his armchair like a baby who's learning how to sit up. Every time someone went by they sat him up again. His fan was too heavy for him; he had difficulty holding it. A postman handed him a telegram. I saw my father, not a little child, crying his heart out.

'Come down and have tea, it'll get cold!'

My mother and my sister were drinking tea. Our courtyard was narrow. Where were the big blinds? Where was the fountain? The pool was empty. The roofs had grown up, I couldn't see the sky from my window any more. The terrace was no more than a pocket handkerchief. In the corridor I could touch the ceiling. A load of sand was piled up where there used to be jasmin.

'Mum! Why did you cut down the trellis?'

'Have you blocked up the fireplace in the prayer room? Why?'

My sister had a far-off look and my mother looked drawn. They exchanged a silent glance. My mother raised to her lips the last remaining china cup. The sideboard which was decorated with two snakes has been sold too. The tiles on the house were slipping and the gutters worn. The little stream had become a ditch full of stones.

In the park even the cypress was dead. The cast-iron railings which went round the park had been pushed over. In the cemetery the women were talking too loud, they were marrying their daughters to soldiers come down from the maquis and, sitting on the graves, they told of the exploits of their future sons-in-law.

'Mum, if we left, this is where all our family is buried.'

'Where would we go? The latest is a month old...'

'Let's go and have tea or a drop of milk.'

My mother was alone, you could hear people going by over-

147

head. You got to that damp room by the sewers like the rats. It was a grave in the middle of the town, that's where she was hiding. In the daytime she would go and search for food, she would leave her hole in the depths of that casbah which she'd never seen except in a dream.

She was climbing up stones as if they were steps, clinging onto the earth on the hillside. It was five o'clock in the morning. A man came up who wanted to kill her and steal her things. She dropped everything, then she went back to the hole where the toilet was a ditch hidden by a rusty iron plate. In the evening when you wanted to pee you watched the rats going by.

My mother had the same dream every night. She was in prison, surrounded by criminals: women who kill a man whenever they get the chance. During these nights she would see a vast crowd of men dressed in black; they pulled her along by the chains on her feet.

She had been condemned to several months imprisonment because she had dared to say that she was the owner of her house and that no one had the right to make her leave it.

'What do you mean, owner? Everything belongs to the people from now on.'

The people, an unclean butcher who had bought the members of the tribunal and the police with legs of lamb in order to take my childhood home for himself.

I escaped early that morning and took a fast train. It stopped just before the sea. At Mamessa's bedside I took in her last words.

'Now I can die in peace. Look after this box.'

I left, clutching the object in my hand. It was a little silver box with mother of pearl on the lid, a name was engraved on it: Dr Maler. I walked in the night for a long time, in that misty town where lights were rare. On a road forbidden to pedestrians a taxi stopped:

'I want to go to the sea, Monsieur.'

After several kilometres the taxi left me near the sea wall. The beach was deserted and the waves stormy. I sat down on the wet sand with a light high above me. I opened the little box, there was a shining bracelet, a little girl's bracelet with two snakes' heads meeting, inscribed: to Lallia.

I slipped down to the water's edge, hugging the little box. I stretched out and the waves covered me, I wasn't cold. I saw myself in a boat going from port to harbour, I would hang about on the wet pavements in a town in the morning while the fishermen pulled live fish out of their crates. I would sleep in stations, sitting opposite morning coffee and a croissant, searching amongst the passing faces.

When I woke up I was in a room. I was surrounded by women who were warming my feet. Then a blue car came to pick me up. It took me to a big house for children who'd lost their fathers. Some of them are fifty years old. They cut my hair. I don't have long hair falling down my back, bouncing as I walk, any more. There are doctors in this big house.

'Is that all you have to tell me?'

'I can tell you about the nightmare I had last night, doctor.'

A taxi was waiting for me below. The driver looked like the soldier from the war memorial.

A light illuminated his cap, as if the light came from the cap itself. It frightened me, I felt threatened. I'd nothing to pay him with. He won't leave without his money. He was watching me. I searched desperately for a way to escape him. My things weren't in my bedroom any more, only a little lamp remained, which was still lit. Suddenly I was back in the street. I left my sister and Boudi, my fish, as security. I don't know how I did it, I ran up and down the stairs. From the stairwell of the block of flats, I watched the taxi. He was still there, like a statue. He thought I was still in the bedroom. He'd been waiting calmly for a long time. I was afraid for my little sister, I had to save her. I couldn't go and leave them alone, it was my fault that they were shut up in there.

Outside it was dark. All the lights in the houses were off. People were sleeping. The taxi was still there, you could see it from here. He was patient, he was waiting. I couldn't go back now, I stayed there hidden behind a wall, I watched him. He'd been there for quite a few nights. I never saw daylight, one night followed another without a break.

149

Then I was back in my bedroom again. The taxi was still there, then suddenly, a light flashed out of the sky. A missile, like a ship from outer space, was hurled in the direction of the taxi, an extraordinary blue light lit up my bedroom, and then nothing. I got up and went towards the balcony. I was in my bedsit, I could see a modern block of flats not far from there. The road was quiet. I went back to bed. It still wasn't daylight.